Pig and other stories

PIG
and other stories

ANTONY LAMBTON

Constable · London

First published in Great Britain 1990
by Constable and Company Limited
10 Orange Street London WC2H 7EG
Copyright © 1990 Antony Lambton
ISBN 0 09 470120 2
Set in Linotron 11pt Sabon by
CentraCet, Cambridge
Printed in Great Britain by
St Edmundsbury Press Limited
Bury St Edmunds, Suffolk

A CIP catalogue record for this book
is available from the British Library

Contents

Author's Note

Five stories are based on fact. In the sixth, *Pig*, I have dealt with the evasion of responsibility and a shutting of eyes to the attempted extermination of the Jews in Europe. I have chosen an entirely imaginary Englishwoman's behaviour to illustrate the point that Germans were not alone in their guilt.

Hans

In the winter of 1942, the coupling of the last coach on a German hospital train returning from the Russian front to Berlin snapped in a conquered Polish area. The thirty-three wounded officers in their bunks and the two hospital orderlies were used to stoppages, and had no idea of the calamity.

Half an hour later, the senior officer, Colonel B. von B. in Thurn, noticed an uncomfortable fall in the temperature and shouted to the junior orderly to find out what had happened. Little black-haired, five foot Wilhelm Brech scuttled off. He returned trembling, and whispered in a nervous voice: 'We are separated from the main train; it's gone.' The Colonel immediately ordered the two other mobile senior officers to come to his bunk to discuss plans. The situation was serious. Contact between the coaches was spasmodic. They might not be missed for two or three hours. Although it was only twelve thirty, the northern days were short. Darkness would soon fall and unless they took immediate steps the coach could be rammed by a train coming from either east or west. Unfortunately they had come to a standstill on a short portion of a single track; the second line had been sabotaged by the partisans.

The Colonel issued the following orders. The two orderlies should immediately issue all available blankets and rugs to wounded officers, who could also warm their bodies with great coats. But no military apparel was to be covered. The two orderlies would then each take a red flag and two lanterns and walk two thousand paces down the line in opposite directions and place one lantern on a hand-built snow base. Afterwards, one should walk eastwards, the other, westwards, along the centre of the line until they came to a station or signal box. They would wave the red flag in daytime, the second lantern after darkness. The Colonel barked out his orders, the orderlies saluted and hurried off. Messages were written in Polish and German informing station masters and signal men of the coach's position; they stressed the possibility of wounded officers dying of cold, at the hands of partisans or through a collision with other trains.

In five minutes the orderlies returned. The senior, a blond Bavarian, Corporal Hans Frederich, stood to attention, cleared his throat and said, 'Sir, we have no red flags.' The Colonel snapped, 'Major Brest haemorrhages all day. Cut two sections of his blood-stained linen and tie them to your fixed bayonets.'

A few minutes later the two men, muffled in great coats and ear-flapped headgear, stepped down on to the line and stood gasping in the icy, misty, faintly sunlit air.

'Goodbye,' said Hans, trying to speak in a friendly voice to Wilhelm, who nodded miserably. Then they walked off in opposite directions. They were dissimilar. Hans was a farmer's son, hampered by short-sightedness; this necessitated thick glasses which resembled the bottom of bottles. He could see best at oblique angles. A tall, strong, reliable, silent man of twenty-eight, he had worked hard all his life and was in love with his wife, a stout, blond girl, the same age as himself, called Elsa. They had two children, a boy of five and a girl of four.

Hans thought himself good-natured, although it always gave him pleasure to cut a calf's throat or finish off a badly castrated lamb. He was aware he had a dangerous temper. At the moment he was looking forward with intense pleasure to ten days' leave with his family in his beloved Bavaria. He licked his lips at the thought of his wife and imagined her for a moment unfastening her twin pigtails before climbing on to their bed. He had not been on leave for two years.

The junior orderly, Wilhelm Brech, was a whining, complaining, undersized little man with lank, dark hair, a narrow face and receding chin. He always believed himself misused. His prototype is still to be found in every European country, often in prisons, complaining about their bad luck.

Four years before Herr Himmler had made an unexpected, informal goodwill recruiting visit to his mountain home town. To give a good impression, the head of the SS left his armed escort at the bottom of the hill. Wilhelm had welcomed him enthusiastically, cheering his statement 'It is necessary to remove blood-sucking Jews from Germany'. Only two years before he had noticed his mother had in her rages stopped referring to her husband's Jewish grandmother. Wilhelm told himself she had lied out of spite. He wondered incessantly if the neighbours had heard and remembered her rantings. Luckily, his parents – his father was a lame dustman – had only moved into the town a few years before, but everybody knew everything in a community like theirs. Whenever Wilhelm allowed himself to think of his alien blood it increased his loathing of Jews. He wholeheartedly supported Herr Hitler and his programme. The new Nazi youth uniform made him feel important.

As Himmler passed out of the gates to drive down the mountain Wilhelm and four other youths had followed his car, cheering. This amused the onlookers; the boys looked comic running with their right arm aloft in the Nazi salute. One of them fell over, three gave up. Wilhelm alone ran on. Going around the second turn Himmler's car hit a stone, lurched sideways off the road and hung in bushes tenuously clinging to the hillside. Wilhelm dropped his right hand and ran forward. The branches were beginning to waver under the weight of the large Mercedes. The boy tried hard to open the door; it was stuck. A furious voice shouted at him to get a stone and knock the handle down. He did as he was told and handed the great man down on to the road. A moment later the car and its driver tumbled down the mountain. This piece of good fortune altered his life. The SS leader made a note of his name in a little black book.

Wilhelm eagerly awaited a summons to Berlin. Nothing happened for two years. Then two Gestapo officers drove up the hill to inform the Mayor that Jewish houses had to be marked with crosses, and those with one-sixteenth Jewish blood were to be classified as aliens. Dismay was shown on many faces when the order was read out on the steps of the town hall. Trading with Jews had been discouraged for years, but on that isolated hill top no-one had paid much attention to laws. But now a list was to be displayed naming the new enemies of the Reich. When he heard the announcement Wilhelm trembled and swore under his breath at his father for allowing his mother to ruin her son's life. His bitter thoughts were interrupted when a corporal bellowed out his name and told him to immediately report to the Captain in the Mayor's parlour. Wilhelm thought his heart would stop. Was he going to be shot? He thought of running; there was nowhere to run. His boots seemed to be filled with lead as he walked up the steps and gave his name to a corporal. He was told to wait. Later he was led into a large room. The Captain sat at a table writing, ignoring Wilhelm as he stood to attention, shivering with terror, cursing his parents. At last his judge looked up. 'Wilhelm Brech?'

'Yes.'

'You are lucky. Our great leader, SS Himmler, with his typical affection for the German people, remembered your name and the service you did him two years ago.' The Captain stopped and stared at him before continuing in a cold voice. 'He has also discovered you have Jewish blood. He is, however, prepared to forget your filthy strain because you saved his life. But you cannot stay in this town – you are to leave with me and join the SS but will serve as a private in the medical corps. Keep that secret, understand? Remember, you must now consider yourself a pure Aryan and help the Führer to rid the country of your race.' The Captain added in a slower voice: 'Your origins will not be forgotten. Be loyal or you will suffer in the same way as other Jews. Before you leave it is your duty to write down the names of any of them in this town omitted from this list.' He handed him a sheet of paper.

Wilhelm looked at three names and quickly added another two, paused and added a third, not a Jew, but a schoolboy enemy, a bully. The Captain looked pleased, dismissed him and told him to be ready in half an hour.

His battalion was stationed near Berlin. From then onwards he became openly anti-Semitic and went round with a gang of boys who enjoyed pushing old Jews off the pavements, kicking them and spitting in their faces. When possible they went to the station to laugh at families being sent off to the new resettlement camps: their parcels, signs of innocence, particularly amused them. When war broke out he hated his job as a medical orderly and was terrified of being sent to the front line. At the same time he was furious at missing promotion. The last straw was his posting to Russia. He felt Herr Himmler had betrayed him. He wished he had left him in the car.

Then his morale was boosted by an order to secretly report to a colonel of the SS. Once again he stood shivering before a desk. The colonel paid no attention but read a file. After five minutes he looked up and said in a cold voice: 'Wilhelm Brech, this is a record of your conduct. It is not altogether satisfactory. You have publicly stated your resentment at your future appointment as a train orderly. You are a fool and I am tempted to cancel it and send you as a stretcher carrier to the eastern front.' He picked up the file again and read it, frowning. Wilhelm was certain they were going to deliberately ensure that he was killed. His body felt cold and he smelt himself. At last his tormentor looked up, smiled and said: 'But, my little Jewboy, we will give you one more chance. You will travel on the trains and report any conversations of the wounded officers concerning the Reich. Try and overhear the late night conversations of senior officers. Always carry with you a towel or hot water as an explanation of your presence in the corridor. You must succeed. It is your last chance.'

As he walked slowly down the railway line he reflected bitterly that everybody was against him. The week before, when he was doing his duty and listening, his head to the door crack, to a conversation in a brigadier's cabin, he had received a terrific kick on his behind which sent him sprawling down the passage. It had come from a captain with his arm in a sling, who told him to stand to attention while he was reported for spying. He shook when he heard the brigadier shout: 'He is not a spy – he is a bloody SS plant!' The voices dropped to whispers. A few moments later the captain came out and shouted for a lieutenant who could only walk with crutches.

The two of them told the other orderly to tie belts tightly around Wilhelm's arms and body, pinioning him. He was then kicked and pushed by crutches down the passage to an outside door and told that unless he promised to give up spying and kissed the lieutenant's remaining foot he would be thrown out of the train. He bent down and kissed the foot and was kicked on the head by the captain. Then he was forced to put his head down the lavatory and one of them urinated on him. He was ordered to stay where he was and his tormentor walked off laughing. His colleague Hans had finally undone the belts and sponged his face. Wilhelm would never forgive them for having tortured and mortified him. Now the devilish officers had sent him out just before darkness. He cheered up: he would report the brigadier for cursing the Führer.

Suddenly the sun disappeared. As he walked eastwards to set up a lantern he shivered with fear and rage. Looking nervously around he saw on one side of the railway an endless plain, its monotony occasionally broken by distant farms and cottages. On his right the railway line was bordered by a forest of fir trees, loaded with snow which frightened him by sliding off the branches with rustling thuds. He looked fearfully at the dark trees, the home of Polish partisans, filthy Jews, and, it was said, parachuted Russians. He took slower, shorter steps, aware the enemy was on the look-out for single men to catch and torture. Once, peering suspiciously down a long forest ride, he saw to his horror a black form slowly crossing the snow! Was it a deer? A bear? A man? If so, had he been seen? He felt dizzy with fear and his heart thumped at the idea of being tortured. Although he had walked only eight hundred paces he decided to leave his lantern and turn back before it was too late. But how could he pass the train? If he was seen, the Colonel would have him shot. He decided to creep along the centre of the line beneath the carriages and catch up with Hans. The idea of the big Bavarian's company was reassuring. He would not have to face the terrifying darkness alone. He looked down the line and saw patches of mist creeping up from the forest. Panic magnified them. How easy it would be for the partisans to creep up on him. This idea helped him to persuade himself that anyway the first train would come from the west. Hurriedly he collected a few handfuls of snow, looking all the time at the forest, trod them down, banged the lantern crookedly on top and ran as hard as he could towards the stranded carriage.

Creeping under the carriage was easier than he had feared and did not take long. Standing up, he shook himself, praised his cleverness and peered down the line through the mist patches. No sign of Hans. Frightened, he started to walk quickly westwards. After a few minutes, he saw a light in the distance. He walked even more quickly and only stopped when he reached a well-moulded, firm snow tower with a flickering lantern buried firmly on its top. He put his hands over his eyes and stared down the line hoping to see a tall figure. The line was empty. Possessed again by panic, he hurled his second lantern down the embankment into the deep snow, and started to run, praying to God, whom he seldom remembered, for a glimpse of Hans. He began to pant with terror and was beginning to despair when he saw him in a gap in the mist, a quarter of a mile ahead, striding along, his red flag waving proudly on his rifle, his lantern swinging in his hand.

'What a fool,' he thought. 'The partisans will see him, us!'

The sweat was freezing on his face when he reached his companion but he was so relieved to have company that he ignored the cold stare of contempt on the Bavarian's face, and said feebly, his eyes averted, that he had left the lantern on a high snow base. Hans wiped his glasses and looked out of the corner of his eyes at Wilhelm. He saw he was lying and asked, 'Are you sure you set your lantern between the lines? Go back. You are lying.'

'No.'

'Can't you realise a train may come from the east?'

Wilhelm made no reply, looked at the ground and marched on, shivering each time he looked at the forest and jumping at the sound of snowfalls from the trees. When he was told he would be put on a charge he shrugged his shoulders. When he was ordered to turn back, he walked on. Hans shrugged his shoulders; there was nothing he could do. Suddenly Wilhelm's long nose caught a faint sickly smell. He paused for a moment and then with excited pleasure ran forward and seized Hans' arm. He was shaken off roughly but he was too excited to notice and shouted, 'Jews: Treblinka, Auschwitz, burning Jews!'

Hans was annoyed. His youth in the country had made him conscious of every sort of smell and when he passed a farm his nose told him what animals were kept there. Now this little beast had noticed a smell before him; it was irritating. He lifted his head. It was true. There was a faint smell of decay. He stood still. Like every German in the eastern army he knew about the extermination and burning of the Jews in Auschwitz. The alteration of military train schedules to fit in with Jewish shipments was a constant source of irritation to the army. It infuriated soldiers that forward positions in urgent need of supplies were kept short owing to the interruption of the military timetable to Treblinka, the mainline station by Auschwitz. Troops looking out of the train window as they passed through the junction often saw trucks arriving stuffed with Jews. A friend of Hans had told him his train had stopped for repairs in the station; trucks from the west had drawn in, the doors opened and Jews had tumbled out, covered with excrement, pale, clinging to pitiful, soiled packages. Ukranians had whipped the younger Jews back into the trucks to pull the dead out and lay them down in two piles. The account had offended Hans' sense of order, but his placid face had not shown his thoughts. He did not like Jews himself, and could never forget that a twenty-five year old cousin of his wife's, a young farmer only four farms away, had fallen into the hands of a moneylender and been evicted. Stories about their meanness and cleverness had been told in the winter evenings as long as he could remember. But why not shoot the bad ones in quarries?

He knew about the poison crystals as well; he had heard two Gestapo officers in another train boasting how many Jews they could dispose of in a day. It seemed to him unnecessary to shut naked people up in chambers and kill them slowly while they screamed in agony. He would not mind killing bad men, but he would shoot them, not torture them, unless they had done something wrong, and he could not see that babies could be guilty. And as for the burning, that was messy. He knew how difficult it was to get rid of bones. Recently, pocket books, watches, and other personal effects had been offered to soldiers at the front. It was known they had been stripped from the bodies of dead Jews. A lot of them were snapped up but Hans would not take one; he thought them unlucky.

Wilhelm, on the other hand, grew more and more excited; his nose twitching, he sniffed the air like a dog. They walked on. Hans, trying to be fair, added up the moments his nasty little companion had been away, wishing his fingers were free to count on. But even without them, he reckoned he had been told a lie. Wilhelm could not have walked two thousand paces, made a snow base, set his lantern up properly and caught up with him. Hans was about to lose his temper when a huge explosion made him spin around to see a cloud of steam and sparks rising into the air. He knew at once that the carriage had been hit by an express because Wilhelm had not placed his lantern correctly and given it time to stop. The collision could have been prevented if the little brute had obeyed orders and walked on eastwards with his flag and the second lantern. Hans' suppressed anger exploded; turning, he looked at his companion who, white and shaking, gazed at the steam cloud, eyes flickering, teeth chattering. Hans knew guilt when he saw it. He took Wilhelm's rifle and laid it on the railway track, put his own down and taking Wilhelm's wriggling left arm, turned him half round and hit him with all his strength on the chest. He never liked to hit men above the neck; it could blind them, break their jaws, but if he hit them in the chest he could put everything into the blow. He watched with satisfaction as Wilhelm shot backwards into the snow. Hans walked over and looked down on the body in silence, bent down, lifted it up by the collar as if it was an empty coat and slapped him on each cheek until he came round. Blood ran down Wilhelm's nose and he could not walk for ten minutes. Once his eyes strayed to the rifles and Hans knew the runt would kill him if he could, as he must realise if he was reported he would be shot for disobeying orders. Hans took Wilhelm's rifle, slipped the bolt out, put it in his pocket, and told him to walk ahead. He had to obey but looked with comic hatred at his jailer.

As they plodded on, the air grew darker and the smell stronger. At last the outlines of Treblinka station formed in the mist. Soon they could see the empty platform. As they climbed on to it a train came in and Hans saw in the bright arc lights, white faces peering out of the top of cattle trucks through small barbed wire windows. Obviously it was a cargo of Jews arriving. The Gestapo officers fondled revolvers, their Ukranian henchmen (you could not call them soldiers) swished their whips and stood in worried groups, gazing at the trucks. They ignored the two unknown German soldiers. The doors opened, the groups broke up, and Hans saw a repetition of his friend's story. Grey-faced, haggard, filthy figures fell out of the trucks, blinking, grasping little parcels, begging for water. The Ukranians whipped the young men back to pull out the dead and pile them into heaps. It was impossible to keep order as the platform was crowded with desperate mothers, old women and lost children crying, dead bodies. A terrible sound of wailing filled the air. Hysterical voices shrieked: 'Father!' 'Mother!' Hans compared the chaos to a market day long ago at home when four young bulls escaped. He looked round and could not see Wilhelm. His anger returned. He was not going to let him escape. For the thousandth time in his life he lamented his shortsightedness. It made him slow, angry. At last he saw him standing by a pillar kicking an old bearded rabbi lying on the ground. This upset him. The Jew was an elder of a church and although Hans was a Catholic, he respected such men. The rabbi looked cleaner than his companions. He lay clasping his prayer book with shut eyes, neither shrieking or trying to evade Wilhelm's boots. It would not have been so bad if he had been one of the miserable, skinny little Jews who looked half dead, but he had the well-kept face of a man who should be respected despite his nationality and religion. Hans was annoyed. He strode forward, treading by mistake on something soft, picked up Wilhelm and smashed his nose into his face as he knocked him off the platform on to the railway line.

Hans knew what he had done, once, years before: he had killed an old oxen in a secret competition in the hills. But unfortunately, moving forward to save the rabbi, he had unintentionally trod on a baby, which he saw lying white, feebly wailing by his feet. He bent down to help the little thing; fingers tore at his face. The fury which had made him kill Wilhelm revived and increased when his spectacles were knocked off. He could not see who was attacking him and felt blind, inadequate, furious. In desperation he kneeled down and groped about, while legs and fists kicked and hit him, stoking up his fury.

At last, by a miracle, he found his spectacles unbroken. He fitted them onto his nose and saw his attackers were an old Jewess and a thin young woman lifting up the baby. Without warning she spat in his face and her fingers again scratched at his eyes. For the second time he lost his temper, shoved her away, pulled the baby by the legs out of her arms, and when she rushed at him again, used it as a club to batter her head until she lay still. The old woman stood speechless, her mouth open, her filthy hair dropping down over her hairy old face, looking, he thought, the personification of beastly Jewishness. Should he finish her off as well? But his tension had been eased by killing Wilhelm and the young Jewess. Gently he walked over and put the dead baby into her arms. She looked into his eyes. He saw agony, and, what surprised and shocked him, pity. He turned away, disturbed, and continuing to worry until he was brought before the station CO. He gave an exact account of his actions and showed his lantern and his home-made red flag. Questioned about what had happened to Wilhelm, he answered simply, he had killed him trying to escape when the Jews came. The officer grunted with pleasure; Hans was taken away and locked up. Two days later he was sent to Berlin, where by good luck he was cross-examined by a Bavarian major who understood the straightforward, simple peasant. After praising Hans for killing the Jewess who had attacked him, he gave him a card permitting him to spend the next ten days at home, patted him on the back, shook his hands and said: 'Enjoy yourself.'

Hans thought of nothing during his brief imprisonment but his wife. Again and again he imagined her unloosened fair hair, the feel of her heavy breasts when he put his hands under them, her blue eyes. He dwelt on the golden fair hair on her body, large thighs and legs; he could not wait to hold her in his arms again. The events at Treblinka station became irrelevant; they belonged only to the past.

On his way home Hans changed trains twice. After the last stop before his home station, he opened the window to look out, ignoring the icy cold air and the protests of other travellers, determined not to miss a second of his homecoming. He knew every inch of the countryside surrounding the railway line, and noticed a stone bridge had collapsed and been replaced by iron girders and that four trees had fallen down; one of them lay across meadow land, wasting valuable grass. He sighed at such inefficiency. It should have been cleared away in two days. At last he saw the station and picked out a group; his father, straight-backed, embarrassed, in his Sunday suit, his wife, wearing her national costume and his children, jumping about with excitement. His mother was not there. He knew she would be preparing dinner for his homecoming. He ran to Elsa and clasped her to him, squeezing the breath out of her body before turning to the children and lifting them aloft side by side in front of him; the trick always made them laugh. Then he shook hands with his father without speaking, each gripping as hard as he could. At last Hans gave in, pretending his father had the stronger hold, otherwise the old man would have been offended. They had played the game ever since he was born and although his father must have known his son was far stronger than he was, a false victory always pleased him. They crowded into a farm cart and drove off; everywhere he noticed improvements. 'Things are good,' his father told him: farmers could not produce enough, money came in fast. The war was bad, of course, but it was good for farming. His cousins were coming in the evening; they would have a 'simple meal'. Father and son exchanged smiles, knowing that Hans' mother would rather die than cook a 'simple meal' when her only son came home.

On arrival at the farmhouse Elsa asked her father-in-law to stop at the gate to let Hans run in and see his mother alone in the kitchen. She would have been embarrassed to see her mother-in-law crying. The old woman believed sentimentality was a weakness and did not like being caught when she thought she was looking silly. He tiptoed through the back of the house, opened the doors quietly, and saw with delight the spotlessly clean kitchen. Rows of hams and every variety of sausage hung as usual from the ceiling. His mother stood by the scrubbed pale wooden table scarred by the meat chopper, rolling dough.

At the sight of her son she turned pale, shuffled and stumbled towards him, her hands held out to pull him towards her. She laid her head on his shoulders, whispered hoarsely she had never thought she would see her 'dear boy' again. She thanked God for his goodness; she would donate five times her usual contribution on the following Sunday. Her spasm of delight over, she began to cry. He took out his handkerchief and wiped her eyes four times. She said she was a silly old woman, he must forgive her. He tried to kiss her but she rapped him hard on the knuckles with her rolling pin; saying if he was stupid she would only make a fool of herself again. His wife and family came in; they had been waiting at the door for the right moment. Hans produced his presents from Berlin: a little doll for his daughter, a machine gun which shot bread pellets for his son, a silk scarf for his wife, six thick coloured handkerchiefs for his mother – she despised fine linen – and a large wedge of tobacco for his father who he knew would cut it up into small pieces and make it last for months. He felt himself swelling with pleasure and happiness and the passionate wish to take Elsa up to their bedroom, but he knew he had to wait and glanced furtively at his watch. It was only five o'clock. He decided to kill time by going round the farm with his father to examine minutely the new barn and each cow. That should last till supper time.

As they went out Elsa whispered: 'Only take the children into the barn, and send them home before you examine the cows or they will get up to some mischief. Your father does go on, you know.' He took a child by each hand and saw how proud his son looked. It was Hans' turn to have tears in his eyes.

The barn was dark. Hans had to guess at rather than see his father's improvements: the taps over each water trough, the new stalls for the horses, the labour saving trap doors above the mangers to drop hay through, which saved time and work. He sent the children home and tried to force himself to be interested, but his old resentment of his father's obstinacy asserted itself and although he was pleased to see him fit and making money, he knew he would have spent the money better himself. He wished his father would make way for him. To his surprise the farm, which he had loved and longed for, bored him. He wondered why, as he heard the perfections and faults of each cow. Then he smiled. It was simple; he could think of nothing except being alone with Elsa. During the last few hours he had wanted her with an overwhelming passion. He looked at his watch; in half an hour the examination would be over, and then would come the long meal before Elsa, and peace for his aching body.

Two of Hans' cousins, who had remained on their farm instead of joining the army, were very friendly. Hans agreed with everything they said. His mother was so busy serving the huge meal she hardly sat down. Elsa watched her children gorge themselves before falling asleep. His father sat quietly eating, saying nothing. He seldom showed interest in anything except his farm and had never mentioned the war. Hans had felt suffocated as a young man when he had realised how his father dominated him and refused to listen to any ideas but his own. He knew he was not clever but he could not bear the endless reminders of his father's superiority. He stared at him appraisingly in the way he looked at an old horse, wondering how long it would live. He sighed. Probably he would survive for years. A fuddled idea came into his mind. Elsa and his children would always follow his lead. When his father was old and weak, they would have their way and insist the old man did as he was told.

Hans thought the feast would never come to an end and with difficulty forced himself to eat his favourite delicacies, only to find another large helping on his plate. At last his cousins stood up, banged him on the back and went away. He kissed his mother goodnight, stood up, slapped his stomach with appreciation, shook his father's hand, forced himself to walk slowly upstairs and quietly shut the door. At last he was alone with his wife. Tactfully his mother had put the children's beds in her own room. He pulled his wife towards him, held her six inches away, carefully examining with unwavering concentration every part of her face. She looked back into his glasses; she wished he would take them off as they distorted his eyes into little dark holes a long way away. She had always admired his physical strength, his quiet dignity and had first seen him, without his spectacles, lifting hay on to a huge, three-pronged wooden fork with effortless ease. At once she chose him as the man she wanted to father her children. The next day, when she had seen him wearing glasses, she felt pleased. He was strong, but bad eyes would make him vulnerable and dependent on her. They married, but alas, had only two fine children. His leaves had been few and short but now surely he would make her pregnant again. She felt weak, receptive as he held her in his arms.

At last, when he had memorised all her features, he let her go and turned towards their bed. She waited, knowing what to do. His habits never changed. He took off his boots, socks and shirt, and barechested walked to the side of their wooden bed, sat down and said to her in an unsteady voice: 'Elsa, please take off your clothes, all but your knickers, then put your nightdress on, and hang your plaits over your shoulders and stand with your back to me.' She nodded silently and did as he asked. Methodically he took off his pants and trousers and placed them neatly on a chair. Naked, he jumped into bed, drew the bed-clothes up to his chest and looked at Elsa, standing expressionless, obedient, her back to him. Once during an early leave she had smiled; he had been angry and disappointed. He gazed at her again and told her to untie her plaits. She obeyed. He watched excited but fearful she would change the routine – she had once – it had confused his nightly fantasies for months until he saw her again. He had an ordered mind. She finished undoing her second plait and with both hands pulled her long blond hair behind her, shaking it until it settled. He said in a hoarse voice, 'Take off your knickers.' She put her hands behind her back, lifted up the back of her nightdress and pushed and wriggled them down over her large hips until they fell lightly to the ground. Hans heard the faint rustle and sighed with relief. Everything had gone perfectly.

'Turn round,' he said. She obeyed and saw him fix his spectacled eyes on her crumpled knickers. 'Take off your nightdress.' She obeyed, throwing it on the floor.

Tearing the sheet down he beckoned to her. Obediently she got into bed. He jumped on top of her. She was not allowed to speak but as she threw her arms around him she tried to make him feel he was giving her another child. To him it was perfect; every action of hers had been identical to his dreams. He scratched himself to make sure

28

he was not in bed in an army wooden hut or a train in Russia. After he had made love he lay back, relaxed, reliving every detail. All went well until he got to 'Take off your knickers'. Then Elsa turned into the young Jewess and started to attack him with her finger nails. He yelled and shoved her so hard she shot on to the floor. He jumped out of bed and, to his relief, saw the Jewess turn slowly back into Elsa. They stood naked, he confused and frightened, she placid, trying to understand what had happened. Realising he was upset she climbed into bed, pulled back the sheets, and patted a place by her side. Slowly he climbed in beside her. She put her arm out gently and guided his head on her shoulder. 'Now,' she said, 'tell me what's wrong.' He told her everything that had happened since they had left the train. He described the wretched Wilhelm's cowardly behaviour, the explosion, the arrival of the truckloads of Jews. His disgust at the kicking of the rabbi, Wilhelm's death. The unfortunate maiming of the baby, the mother's attack on him. The loss of his spectacles and temper, the hitting of the mother with the child. His arrest for killing Wilhelm. Then suddenly he hugged Elsa so hard she could not breathe. He whispered: 'I have thought of you every night for months. The happiness of being with you has confused me. Now I mind nothing as I am with you, except killing that girl with the baby, but I told you I lost my temper when she kicked me because I could not find my spectacles, and you know how mad I get without them. But still I wish it had not happened; when I was remembering exactly how I had made love to you – I have to fix every detail in my mind to recall it when I am back in the army – you suddenly turned into the dead baby's mother, that is why I kicked you out of bed. Do you understand?'

Elsa thought for a moment and said slowly, 'I understand. It must be a shock to kill a woman and her baby even if they are Jews. But don't blame yourself for anything, except for losing your temper, which was bad. You only killed that Wilhelm because he was kicking the rabbi while after all, you saved the baby and its mother pain – they would have been stripped naked and gassed. It takes over ten minutes for them to die, my cousin Max was told by a friend in the Gestapo. So, you see, you have saved them from an unpleasant death. Forget them all,' she said, stroking his cheek. 'Your bad temper for once did good.'

Hans felt better. Her common sense had, as usual, reassured him. He studied her again and noticed the lushness of her heavy bosoms. He concentrated on them. She smiled as he took his spectacles off, and when he lay heavy on top of her, whispered, 'Give me a baby like you, exactly like you.' A moment afterwards she screamed in ecstasy, 'Like you, like you, exactly like you.'

Out of the forest

Jan was born in a sporting forest, for centuries the property of a great family, in the western Russian province of Poland. Nine game-keepers guarded the domain which, in that roadless land, stretched for six miles by twelve, circled by a split oak fence. The keeper's business was to kill the smaller vermin, prevent poaching and to keep the larger animals from damaging surrounding crops. A difficult task; the thickets were stuffed with bears, boars and many kinds of deer from every part of the world.

In 1814 the keepers' houses were built, at equal distances from each other, around the perimeter of the wood. Each stood in a clearing of three acres; enough land to allow the growth of corn and vegetables and make the households self-supporting. A cow-house, pig and sheep pens completed the smallholding. In the daytime the domestic animals wandered in the forest, and at night time were locked in.

Jan's mother died at his birth in 1900. He was saved from starvation by a widow whose baby had died. She had no chance of avoiding intimacy with his father, a tall, strong, big-nosed black-bearded man, but she ignored the child after he had left her breast. A good cook, she kept the wooden house clean and neat, but seldom spoke and was considered by the other keepers and their wives to be moonstruck. Often in the long summer nights she would sit on a rough bench under an oak tree, chanting, her eyes lifted to the sky. She never had another child.

As soon as Jan could walk, his father showed him the gates into the forest which became his outdoor home; innocent, without intent to harm, he established a fearless relationship with the animals, who ignored him. One of his first memories was of walking up to a large bear sitting on a fallen tree eating grubs. He never forgot the small, hard eyes and the harsh smell of the large animal. For some time the two looked at each other. Jan never knew what was going on in the bear's mind, but suddenly it shook its head, turned round and walked clumsily away.

When his father heard of the meeting he shook his head and said, 'I understand all the animals in the wood except the bears. They are treacherous creatures. God must have taken care of you.' He crossed himself. 'If not, you are lucky. Avoid the beasts or you will die.'

Jan always listened and obeyed, and never risked going near one of them again. His father taught him to read the different animal tracks on the ground which would tell him where the animals were before the prince's shoots. Occasionally he would wake his son before dawn and lead him silently through the dark trees to the watering holes. They would crouch in silence and watch the animals come in peace to drink. The little boy loved these excursions but often, as he trotted along, he hoped his father would take his hand. He never did.

In the spring and summer evenings they sat in silence, his father smoking his pipe, his gun resting against his chair, always ready to dash out if he heard a shot or unusual sound in the forest. His foster-mother either sat outside or spinning in a corner. The neighbouring keepers and their wives paid occasional visits but seldom stayed long. Jan hated strange women lifting him up and pressing him to them declaring 'what a fine boy' he was. He liked the softness of their breasts, but he always wished to hide behind his father's legs. The boy never heard the word 'love' but later realised he had loved his father with his whole heart.

One day when Jan was five, his foster-mother mysteriously disappeared. He remembered a strange consequence. On either side of the brick fireplace stood two rocking chairs. The night after she vanished his father said calmly, 'You can move the bench now and sit opposite me.'

Jan was surprised; his foster-mother had never sat in the rocking chair. He said nothing but proudly took his new place thinking 'I am a man now'. Women, he decided, often disappeared. His mother had left before he knew her. Now it was his foster-mother's turn. He seldom thought of her again; she had never shown him affection. But he always remembered how she had looked one winter evening. A shot was fired in the wood. His father disappeared. Immediately she dropped her spinning wheel and knelt before the fire. The flames lit up her face, making it red and luminous in places, black in others. He saw with fear her eye-sockets become bigger and emptier; they appeared to be sliding into the back of her head, like dry earth falling into an ant hole. He watched her from his bed in a wooden alcove, lying between two feather eiderdowns. After a time her stillness frightened him and he shut his eyes to avoid seeing her. Twice before he went to sleep he opened them. She still knelt unmoving, gazing into the fire, her black and red face changing shape in the flickering light.

Jan was not unhappy, his love for his father was enough. His pleasure was undiluted when he was praised for spotting the tracks of boars or stags, or when the vegetables grown in his own little garden were said by his father to be the biggest and best in the clearing. At night he would lie thinking proudly of these occasional, never forgotten triumphs.

When Jan was twelve the head game-keeper enrolled

him as an extra under-keeper, putting in his hand two pieces of silver – he did not know what for. He had never left the forest or heard of buying and selling. He was given a small rifle and told to kill jays, foxes, hawks and any animals wounded on shooting days. Previously he had been forbidden to leave the clearing on these days and had wandered worried, uneasy, listening all day for faraway shots.

The morning after his enrolment his father woke him at five o'clock. The pair, carrying leather satchels full of bread and bacon, walked several miles along a rutted, sandy track which ended in a large, round clearing. Although the sun had not risen it was full of groups of strange men wearing belted smocks and high leather boots, talking quietly together. Half an hour later his father told him to follow another keeper and imitate his movements. A horn was blown and all the men started walking to left and right down the track, stopping in turn and standing still until they had formed a line which appeared to stretch endlessly in both directions. At a second blast they moved forward and vanished into the undergrowth. Jan walked a few yards from the keeper, aping him every time he hit a tree or stood still. For a long time the only noise was the tapping of sticks but at last, far in front, he heard shots which, as they walked forward, grew louder and louder. A horn was blown. They walked on a few yards in silence and entered a broad clearing in which men were climbing down ladders from platforms in the trees. Here and there lay dead or dying boars, deer and three bears, soon surrounded by a gaping crowd. He did not have time to examine them, the beaters were called together and marched off, left and right, along another ride. They left behind them the men from the platforms; they wore green hats and shining boots, and stood round a white table

covered with bottles. White-gloved men in brightly coloured coats and white stockings handed round plates piled
with food. The shoot continued. Each drive started and
ended in the same way. Jan could not imagine how the
smart men could eat and drink so often. On the way home
his father said, 'You kept up well.'

His son swelled with pride.

In 1913 Jan took part in twelve shoots. His father told
him at the end of the first day that the smallest man of all
the marksmen, so small you sometimes missed seeing him,
was their Prince, who lived in a castle twenty miles away.
The beautiful woman in a long fur coat, who sometimes
came out with other smart ladies, was his wife. Twice a
marksman was a Russian grand duke, a relation of the
great Tsar, others were German princes; once he was
pointed out a man who had come from over the sea. Jan
asked 'What is the sea?' When his father puffed at his pipe
without answering Jan blushed. He never asked the question again, but wondered for years what it could be. Later
he was told the sea was a great lake. He never saw it.

The next year when they were getting ready for the
shooting season, his father told him war had been declared
and the Tsar was leading Russia to fight against the
Germans. At first it did not seem to make any difference
to their lives but two months later his father shook his
head and said, 'Our armies are falling back, I do not know
what is happening. It seems many men have been killed.
What we are fighting about I do not know.'

Shortly afterwards two dirty strangers walked into the
clearing, one with his arm in a bloody sling. His father
gave them food and a night's shelter. Before they left the
three sat close together talking in low voices. Afterwards
Jan was told that the Prince had left his castle.

Two days later four more strangers carrying rifles
appeared. His father could not understand what they said.

This made them angry; they shouted and threatened him with bayonets. He stood motionless; Jan hoped he would grow up to be as brave, and watched, his heart beating with fear and pride, as his father stood without flinching, ignoring the thrusting blades. The boy could not understand what was happening. Afterwards he was told: 'They are Germans, our enemies. They now live in the Prince's castle.'

Winter set in; father and son remained undisturbed. But in the late spring eight men in uniform rode up to the cottage, looked greedily at the young vegetables and the next day returned with a pony cart and collected them all. His father said nothing, but when they had left, gave his son a spade and the two dug up the earth and sowed seeds. His father said, 'At least they have not damaged the young corn, the vegetables will grow again, the forest soil is rich.'

They were left alone for a few months but at the first snowfall the men returned. His father was ordered to hand over all his guns. He gave them four. They took them away. He asked how he could work without them. His words were translated by a man who spoke Polish and German. He was told, 'You are lucky not to have been shot. You will have to make do with bows and arrows.' The thieves rode away laughing.

His father, for once, smiled, beckoned to his son and lifted him up until he was level with one of the four main cross beams which supported the sloping roof. In it Jan saw a rifle lying in a long hollow. It was the most beautiful gun he had ever seen; made of shining metal and wood, inset with pieces of elephant bone. His father fondled the stock, smiled and said the late Prince had given it to his father, with gunpowder, shot and a ram-rod. It was old and had to be loaded through the muzzle. The powder was weighed before it was rammed down the barrel, followed by a black wad and a round lead ball. Jan was lifted up again and told to put the rifle back exactly where he had found it. It was taken down again three weeks later and his father shot two stags to feed them through the winter.

Two days afterwards the Germans appeared, angry, shouting. A man with a shining spike on his helmet hit his father's face and ordered his soliders into the house with long iron bars and a ladder. Jan's heart sank and he was terrified they would find the secret hiding place.

To his dismay he soon heard shouts of triumph. Shortly afterwards the man with the glistening spike came out carrying the hidden gun, with a look of respect on his face as he caressed the stock. He gave it carefully to a soldier and ordered a pony cart to move forwards. Jan's father was forced to stand in the back. When his hands were roughly pulled behind his back he spoke in a dignified voice to the man with the shining spike, who nodded. His hands were released, he beckoned to his son, lifted him up, although he was fourteen and as tall as himself, kissed him on both cheeks, gripped his back and looked into his eyes as if to tell him he was a boy but now he had to be a man. Suddenly he put him down, looked at the ground, muttered a few inaudible words and placed his clenched hands behind his back. A soldier tied them together. Jan with horror realised his father was helpless and ran towards him. One of the soliders seized him. A rope was tied round his father's neck. The cart was led under a tree. The other end of the rope was thrown over a branch and knotted. A soldier, without warning, fired a gun, the horse lunged forward, his father hung, his legs kicking in the air. A German jumped off the ground and hung on to him. The rest laughed, one of them set the cottage on fire. Without looking back, they rode away.

Jan felt as if he had been hit on the head, but pulled

himself together and ran over to see if his father was alright; the body had ceased to kick, but the neck looked longer, the head was at an odd angle and the face a bluish colour. He shouted, his father was silent and when in desperation he pulled a leg, the body swung towards him; when he let it go it swung away. The boy lay on the ground, thrust his fists into his eyes and made up his mind to leave the clearing. He ran through the wood to a sheltered place in an old oak tree full of brown leaves where he often sat happily listening to the birds, lay down and sobbed; he thought his heart would break.

The next night Jan slept with the cows. Luckily, they had been in the forest each time the Germans came. During the winter he lived lonely, but comfortable, drinking milk and eating bits of lamb roasted over a fire and vegetables which he picked as his father had taught him, from a tunnel he dug beneath the snow.

The next spring the Germans returned. By good fortune he heard them coming. They searched the surrounding woods and drove away all the animals except one nervous cow which Jan caught and led on to an island in a swamp surrounded by high rushes. He built a small shed, roofed and sided it with heather and set up house with the animal, which he fed on hay from the clearing. For the next few months he talked to the cow every night, telling her of his traps for rabbits and birds, or how he had found a patch of wild oats he would cut for her when they were ripe. The animal's passive face made her a sympathetic listener, and stopped him from going mad.

One day in early autumn he woke up to see the bearded, familiar face of a neighbouring keeper who had occasionally visited his father, looking down on him. The man told Jan that to begin with they had given him up for dead but he had been glimpsed in the wood, and all the keepers had been trying to find out where he had hidden himself. Why, he asked, had Jan never come to them, and added, 'I came to your father's clearing four times last winter. I never spoke to you but glimpsed you escaping from your cow-house so I knew you were alright. My wife has been on at me about you. I will have a rest from her tongue when I bring you home.' They took the cow with them; the keeper said he would say he had found it – if questioned – wandering alone in the forest.

The life in the open had hardened Jan's body and a sparse, black beard covered his chin. When they arrived at the keeper's cottage the housewife for a moment backed away from him. She quickly recovered herself, kissed him and asked him why he had behaved like a savage. They would give him shelter but it would not be safe for him to sleep in the house, the Germans occasionally dropped in. The keeper helped him to build a little tree hut outside their clearing in the low branches of an oak with yews growing beneath it. It was invisible and his wife told the boy he could help her with the harvest and the vegetables. 'My husband,' she added bitterly, 'only loves the forest. He will not want to take you with him.'

For a few days Jan, who had been surprised at his warm welcome, was shy and silent, but the motherly woman soon won his confidence and made him realise she was more interesting to talk to than a cow. She understood he was dwelling on his father's death, and instinctively knew it was necessary for him to get rid of his memories. With quiet insistence she made him tell her what had happened, even the terrible moment when he touched his father's leg and the body swung dead in the air. She shook her head when he described his loneliness in the forest and how he had stroked the cow and nestled up against it, grateful for company.

'Oh, you poor boy,' she cried, jumped up, put her arms round his neck and pulled his head onto her shoulder.

'You poor thing, how I hate this war.' From then on it was only a step towards their sleeping together. It was uncomplicated; her husband spent every day and sometimes nights in the forest. Gradually, she, a village priest's daughter, educated him, and taught him to read and write basic Polish so that when the war ended and Poland became an independent country he was – for the countryside – an educated, strong, good-looking young man with a thick, black beard.

I have told Jan's early history because his life in the forest enabled him to live in conditions which would have killed an ordinary man; it also made a decision he had to take later in his life more difficult than it would otherwise have been.

After the war his looks, strength and romantic history made him a figure of interest to the Prince, who on his return to the castle found that the German officers had used pictures for revolver practice, smashed quantities of furniture and hanged three of their private soldiers for stealing a small quantity of silver from a cupboard. Jan was given a job on the home farm and in 1930 was made the organiser of game carts on shooting days.

In that year in a village four miles from the town of Jasionowka he met the daughter of a school teacher – a pretty young Jewish girl, Bathesheba, or Bath as she was called – and decided directly he saw her to ask her to marry him. It did not enter his mind she would refuse. A simple man, he understood they loved each other. When he dutifully told the Prince he was surprised to be told to delay his decision. 'The Jews have always been regarded with loathing in this countryside.' He was also asked if her family agreed. To his surprise they did not. He pined. At last the Prince could no longer bear the giant's unhappiness, and said to him: 'I will arrange it. You have had an odd life, but you are a good workman and half-educated and may be happy with her. But you are not going to become a Jew, are you?'

'No, but my future wife wishes our children to be Jewish. I do not mind; I never had any religion myself.' The prince shrugged his shoulders.

After their marriage Jan was surprised when neighbours no longer asked him to their houses and that the pretty wife of a farmer, with whom he had flirted, told him she was sorry he had made a bad choice. 'You had better watch out, her family will settle like ticks on you, they are a nation of bloodsuckers.' Nothing of the kind occurred. They were perfectly happy. She had three children.

Jan realised he was not as clever as Bath; she understood his honest, simple nature and loved his strong body. Sometimes he would ask her in the evening to read to him improving books. Invariably, after half a page, he fell asleep.

On 5th June 1939 he was called up to serve in the army, but caught chicken-pox at the end of August and the war was over before he had reached his regiment. The Prince had fled to Sweden, this time never to return. The castle became a German SS headquarters. Fortunately, Jan's cottage stood at the back of the stables facing the country-side. His family was ideally hidden.

In 1939 their children, Jacob, Hannah and Rebecca, were eight, four and two. Bath was still a plump, pretty, fair-haired woman, scrupulously clean, a good cook and a strict but loving mother. She did not look Jewish, resembling rather the perfect Nordic type which Hitler was trying to perpetuate in Germany. She was a cuckoo in the nest, as her father and mother, brothers and sisters, all had dark hair; it was a mystery why she was a blonde, but it never troubled Jan or anybody else before the German invasion.

When Jan returned from the army Bath, speaking in a worried voice, said they must discuss the future. 'I will begin by saying I was told by my family not to marry you, but one of my own people, and that I would be unhappy. The advice was wrong. But, owing to my being a Jewess, you will suffer. Hitler hates the Jews, there are terrible stories of Germans killing even babies in Warsaw. My father believes the same thing will happen here and we will be exterminated. Leave me if you wish and go away and work somewhere else. I will understand.'

She sat down and cried. Jan lifted her up, put his arms around her, stroked her head and said, 'My love, I will stay with you. You have made me happy. I know how I am slow, my childhood was hard, you have given me love and children. I am lucky. I could not live if you left me, but you do not look Jewish and Hitler will surely not want to make more enemies. Anyhow, what happens to you, happens to me.'

Bath at once dried her eyes and became practical. 'We are lucky that this house faces the old track leading to Jasionowka, we need not use the road. Unfortunately the children look like my family, but the more I am seen the better, as I look like a German. I have taken Jacob away from school and will teach all the children here and take them to see my family in the winter evenings when it is dark and in the summer by the old road.'

She never went to the synagogue again, but once a month a young rabbi would walk over to talk to her. Jan would leave them alone to pray together. He noticed Bath was always uneasy before and after these visits or if any officers walked past the house. He, on the other hand, did not worry but was always pleased when his wife sang as she did the housework, but in quieter tones than before. She watched the children all the time, and planted a privet hedge on the border of the small garden so nobody could see in.

Jan had already taught Jacob to saw wood and cut down small trees. At the first snowfall, he took him for the first time into the prince's woods to show him the tracks of different animals. The little boy was quick to learn. Remembering his own youthful longings, Jan held his son's hand.

One night in December an event occurred which momentarily eased their fears. An SS lieutenant general was expected at the castle. Jan was woken up at two o'clock by a loud knocking on the door. Bath sat upright, white, shaking. He went to the window and called out, 'Who is that?' A torch was shone in his face and a voice shouted, 'I'm from the castle, you clod. It's snowing like the devil. The General is lost. Get your sledge out quickly and see if you can find him. Our vehicles are hopeless in this snow.'

Jan said he would come to the castle as soon as he could, but they must understand he had to dress, to harness his horse, and put it in the shafts. The unseen man, without answering, walked away.

Half an hour later, he drove into the castle courtyard to find vehicles drawn up against the walls, completely covered with snow, which was falling in huge flakes. He looked up at the sky and smelt the air. It was a bad storm and would continue. Outside the shelter of the walls the snow was drifting, a man would have a poor chance on a night like this. Sentries refused to let him in, but at last an officer appeared and told him the general had vanished on the main road from Jasionowka, only two and half miles away. Jan knew it by heart. He nodded his head and was about to start when a collaborator, a fat, Polish doctor, came bundling up with a medicine chest and a bottle of vodka and, in a frightened voice, asked him if he could come. Jan said in a furious voice, 'No'. The fat man looked relieved, threw the vodka and medicine chest into the sled and hurried back into the castle.

In the open country the snow was blowing diagonally, and lay a foot deep. Jan's mare had hard work forcing her way along, but it was, at the worst, only a short journey and he knew all the places where a track could be mistaken for a road. He had a shovel in the sledge and after five hundred yards they reached a turning. He stepped down and shovelled aside the drift to see if it covered wheel tracks on pressed snow. There were none. He knew four other places where the general's car could have turned off. The first two had no wheel tracks, at the third he found them. Taking his horse by the head, he led it at a slow pace along a snow-covered lane which he knew by heart.

After two hundred yards, he reached a slope. On its left, lying on its side, having turned over twice, a half-buried car lay against a tree. Jan struggled through the snow and, tugging open one of the front doors, saw two bodies. He pulled out the top one with difficulty. It was very heavy. The man was dead. He put his hand in front of the second man's mouth. He was dead as well. In the back a body was slumped sideways; he knew it was the general by his cap and uniform. He put his hand over his mouth and felt warm breath. He hauled him out, dragged his heavy body through the snow into the sledge, poured vodka between his lips and set off for the castle.

The journey back was easier. Despite the drifting, the blurred imprints of his sledge on the surface remained. When they reached the road the mare lifted her head and, as if guided by the smell of home, plodded through the snow, which was falling so quickly her ears, from the driving seat, were invisible. Twice in the next half hour Jan poured more vodka between the unconscious general's lips. At the castle, lights shone and officers ran out to carry the unconscious man to bed. Jan was hit on the back and the drunken doctor tried to pour brandy down his throat. He refused, thinking of his horse standing, without a blanket, in the snow. Taking the tired animal to the stable, he rubbed it down, put a thick rug over its back, gave it three shovelfuls of oats and went to bed. Bath was lying awake with her eyes open. He told her what had happened. She gave a sigh and said, 'We are lucky. Perhaps God will help us.'

Four days later Jan received a message to report to the castle at ten o'clock the next morning. He put on his smartest suit and best boots and walked through the deep snow into the castle courtyard. He was surprised how stupid the Germans were; instead of using a heavy roller on the snow they had shovelled the drifts off the road. It would blow back in patches every night. It was obvious they were ignorant men.

He was taken into a small room and was surprised and shocked to see a painting of the prince looking down at him from above the mantelpiece and below it a large photograph of the princess, in furs, standing on a path in the wood, exactly as he remembered her. Jan stood still, gaping, until the general stood up, put out his hand, and, speaking in bad Polish, thanked him for saving his life and asked him how he had managed to find them. Jan said simply he knew the only places where it was possible to leave the road. The general asked where he was brought up. Jan told him of his life in the forest. He was at once asked about his job as a young keeper.

'Did you track animals?'

'Yes.'

The general looked interested and told him he could be useful. 'The woods and swamps are so large and thick, men are hiding in them. You may be employed as a well-paid tracker. Thank you for saving my life.'

He gave Jan a one hundred mark note, shook his hand and dismissed him.

Bath questioned him minutely about every detail of the conversation and jumped when he said proudly, 'The general offered to use me as a tracker.'

'You did not agree?'

'Why not? I am good at tracking.'

'Don't you see who you will be asked to track down? Many of us have escaped into the forest.'

'I would never track them.'

'I know,' she said. 'I know you won't, but now it is going to be difficult to say why.' She sat silently looking at the floor. He felt inferior to her and stupid not to have thought before he had spoken.

Every time Bath went with her children to visit her family she returned white and trembling with terrible stories of the massacre of Jews all over Poland and the organisation of ghettoes even in country towns. She sobbed as she told Jan that the Germans had blockaded families in their houses, set fire to them and shouted with laughter when mothers clutching their babies had jumped out of windows. Jan smoked his pipe and listened, thinking it unlikely men could behave like that, but then he remembered how they had hung his father.

His rescue of the general made them safe for a few months. During this period he came at last to believe that Hitler intended to kill all the Jews in Poland. Everybody spoke openly about the dreaded concentration camps, at which trucks of dead and half dead Jews arrived daily from distant countries. Bath fainted when she heard the news that the Germans were making registers of the Jews in all the villages around Jasionowka.

She had stopped singing and often seized her children and kissed them. She was sure they would be discovered, for the Germans always managed to get hold of Jewish informers even in the closest knit communities, and torture them into giving the names of anyone who had their fatal blood.

The summer of '42 was terrifying. Jews were daily massacred or disappeared. Bath said, 'It is only a matter of time before we are killed.' Jan was silent and at last said, 'You may be right, the Germans are looking at me in a funny way and never mention, like they used to, how I saved the general from the snow.'

He put his pipe down. 'Do you think you could live in the forest? I know a place we could hide. When I take my week's holiday next month I will go and make us a house.'

'It is not possible. I am four months pregnant. How could I bring up a baby in such a place?'

'Why did you not tell me?'

'Because I don't want to have it. Because I have tried to lose it. Why should I have a baby who will be killed? You must go, and take Jacob; we could have all gone but for this cursed child.' She hit her stomach with both fists.

Jan thought how unlucky it was that Bath was having a baby. For some time, in the back of his mind, he had been thinking of living with his family in the forest and had pictured their hand-made cabin, in the rushes in the middle of the swamp. If he had survived, they could as well and what was more, his children would not be alone as he had been, with nobody to talk to, which had made him slow-minded. Now the baby had ruined everything.

On December 20th 1942 Bath gave birth to a girl, Susannah. Instead of loving her child she found herself hating her, hoping she would die and allow them to escape to what she now thought of as a garden of Eden. As it was, the news grew daily worse. The local Jewish leaders were told to prepare quotas of those who could be sent to Treblinka.

The new SS colonel in the castle sent for Jan and asked

him if he was married to a Jewish girl. He said 'yes' and was given a chance, due to his loyal behaviour in the past, of renouncing her. He refused. He was told a guard would be put on his house and that it was well known it was his intention to escape. 'Do not do that but leave your wife and family. If you insist on remaining married to a Jewess, you become a traitor and your family will end up in Treblinka. Get out.'

On the 1st of January the Jewish authorities in Jasionowka were ordered to publish an exportation list of a thousand Jews. It consisted of a cross section of the community, including young and old. Bath was told the colonel had insisted her family should be put on the list. She told Jan and added, 'I have found out we are to go in sledges which will mean we will pass your forest. Escape with Jacob. Why should we all die? I am resigned. There are no tears left in me. I am numb, but you must escape.'

'No.'

'Well, think about it,' she begged, pulling at his arm, 'and if during the drive you see an opportunity, jump with Jacob. What good does it do for all of us to die?'

'No,' he said. 'I cannot leave you and the baby.' For the first time in their married life Bath screamed at him, 'Can't you see I regard the little wretch as a murderer? I tried to kill her last night and lifted up a pillow. Without her we could have all escaped, but I could not do it.' She ran out of the room.

The waiting seemed endless; Jan cut logs. It did not help. He could not escape misery or sleep at night. If he tried to comfort Bath, she repulsed him, or sat or lay as still as a dead woman. The children seemed subdued. Did they know they were going away? Were they unhappy? Did they realise they were going to die? They did not dare to ask him.

The night before their final journey a sledge drew up

50

before Jan's cottage. Two Germans stepped out. One of them walked towards the castle, the other opened, without knocking, the front door, announcing calmly his name was Karl Heinkle and he was to drive them the next day to Treblinka. The whole party was due to leave Jasion-owka at six in the morning. He would spend the night on the sofa unless they had a spare room. He also stated calmly he would have supper with them that evening and produced a bottle of schnapps. Bath thought, although plump, he was a good-looking man, and that it would be nice to kiss him. She was appalled at herself and knew she was going mad.

During supper Jan felt as if he was dreaming. Was it possible to eat with a man who was going to drive his family to their death the next day? What made the situation odder was that Heinkle had brought a 'pleasant surprise', strings of frankfurters, white Munich sausages and a box of special mustard. He stated the exact time the sausages should be boiled. Heinkle smacked his lips as he ate and drank. At last he finished, pushed back his chair, took out a notebook, slapped it down on the table, opened it and turned over the pages. The children had been sent to bed. Bath had been unable to resist giving each of the three older children two frankfurters. It would be their last good meal. She remained dry-eyed.

After Heinkle had studied his notes and refilled his glass, he said to Jan, 'I see you are making a martyr of yourself. You are a fool. Why die when you don't have to?'

Jan said in a tired voice he could not live without his family. Karl shrugged his shoulders. 'You are mad; I would be pleased to be rid of a Jewish family.' Looking out of the corners of his eyes, he added, 'I believe the general would still let you off if you changed your mind. There are plenty of German widows about nowadays. You could take your pick. You obviously like fair women,' he added, pointing at Bath. She stared unbelievingly at a man who could calmly discuss her husband's future wife the day before he was going to drive herself and her children to be gassed.

Heinkle helped himself to another drink. 'I can't say I would have chosen my job. You know, it is unpleasant driving people who you know will not come back, but I have to obey orders. I don't really know why the Führer decided to do away with you all. It's a messy job, you know.' He swayed a little. 'A messy job, but I am glad it is nothing to do with me, the final killing, I mean.' He swayed again. 'I would like you to know that I have never profited from the doomed. Some of my charges offer me watches and rings, I do not know why, but I always refuse them, or any of your folks' belongings after they are dead. But there is one thing I will do. That is to take gold and leave you half of your hoard. You can bury the rest in your garden. This woman can stay with me to see I do not know where you are hiding it.'

He winked at Jan, who paid no attention. A cunning look came into Heinkle's dull eyes as if he had seen a way of solving the problem. He spoke slowly, his head on one side. 'If you have hidden your treasure in your garden, be wise and live. Jump off my sledge. I won't see.'

Jan said, 'I have no gold.' The German shook his head in anger. 'Stupid pig.' He closed his eyes, opened them and said drunkenly, 'They say we should be through the job of doing away with you all next year. I don't know why I have talked to you. It is against orders. You are meant to believe you are going somewhere in the west, but I know by your faces you are aware of your fate. I have four children like you. Your trouble is you are too clever. Now my children are not clever, they like eating but they do not read except what they have to at school. After all, they have to do what they are told. I suppose your children read, don't they?'

Nobody answered.

'Well, I'm sure they do. All those prayers, you are always mumbling. But then you should not, you know, have had so many money-lenders in Germany, swindling the peasants; or set England and America against us; or joined the international conspiracy. I am sorry to drive you tomorrow, but I am angry with you.' He banged the table with his fist. After a moment's silence he said, 'It has upset me that your children are the same age as mine, and the same size, except that they are Jewish. Take the food out of the room. I am tired, but I am efficient. I have set my alarm at four o'clock. I notice you have packed, but please remember when you go to bed tonight that I am put out.'

'Thank you,' said Bath coldly.

'Good night,' said the German.

Neither Bath nor Jan slept and twice heard Jacob sobbing in the next room. Once when the little boy's tears sounded as if they came from beyond desperation, she seized her husband's arm. 'Escape tomorrow. Promise me. Do not say a word to anybody, but escape with Jacob.' Jan sighed and turned his back. She wished she had a long knife to drive into it.

Bath had a bath at four o'clock and gave her children hot tea and two white sausages which the German had failed to eat the night before. It seemed petty but she hoped he was expecting them for his breakfast. She dressed the children in their thickest clothes. By 4.45 they were ready to go. She took their guest coffee on the sofa and woke him up; his alarm had failed to go off. Despite her knowledge of his cold-blooded plans the rules of hospitality were embedded in her mind.

Jan had thought he would be miserable to leave the

house in which he had been perfectly happy for ten years, but he felt no emotion. As they bumped off he saw two tears run down Bath's cheeks and freeze before they were level with her mouth. At Jasionowka other families were crammed into their sledge – one of a large convoy.

The journey took ten hours. The sledges, despite appeals, never stopped except to change horses and the children fouled their clothes. The smell was bad. When they arrived at Treblinka they found the roads crammed with Jews. They were herded into a transit block which had hundreds of dirty mattresses scattered about the rooms; they were told to use them.

The next morning they were marched into what they guessed was the forecourt of the gas chambers. Many of the women started to scream and cry. To stop the noise Ukranians walked among them with whips. When the children whimpered their mothers and fathers were hit. A man, through a loudspeaker, shouted out orders that all the prisoners should undress and place their clothes and belongings in neat piles. A few of the women had rings tugged off their fingers and earrings torn out of their ears. Some shrieked with pain. The Ukranians beat them. Bath refused to speak, hold Jan's hand or pay attention to her children.

As the doors opened she turned on him fiercely, 'Why did you not escape with Jacob? No-one would have blamed you. I would have died happy.'

'No,' he said. 'I could not have lived without you.'

'Fool!' she shrieked at him.

That was her last word before they were pushed into a white-tiled, cement-floored chamber. Reluctant screamers had to be flogged and pushed inside. Crystals were poured down the columns. Despite their determination Jan and Bath's personalities disintegrated, they fought to get out of the doors when the poison fumes reached them, and joined a mob trampling on the weakest. After ten minutes, an SS man who had calmly examined the turmoil through a thick glass porthole, gave a sign. The doors were opened. Everyone in the chamber was dead.

Karl Heinkle shook his head several times that evening. He simply could not get over the fact that he had been instrumental in the killing of a married couple with four children the same age as his own. It did not seem right; the fact that they were Jews did not diminish his uneasiness. He drank a whole bottle of schnapps and had a nightmare.

Two mornings later he drove another convoy of Jews to their death, and felt very relieved that no family in his sledge reminded him of his own children, but he still could not get Jan's family out of his mind.

On his next leave, when his children clustered round him shouting for their presents, he burst into tears.

'Oh, my little ones, thank God you are not Yids, I could not have borne to lose you. You must all swear to me that, whatever happens, you will only marry Germans, never Jewesses, however rich or beautiful. Oh, oh, oh.' He continued to sob, tears running down his fat cheeks.

'How I love you, my plump, good little ducklings. I want you to know that your father would die for you.'

His wife thought she was lucky to have married such a tender-hearted man.

The axe-man

On the 18th of November 1855 the Grand Duke of Werthiem and eight friends spent an unforgettable day shooting on his estate in the Black Forest. Everything went well. It was a crisp October day, the sun shone providing pleasant but not tiring warmth. The Grand Duke shot seven boars and each of his companions at least two. No comparable day could be remembered by the oldest keeper, and that evening the grand ducal party celebrated the event in his hunting lodge at the edge of a village above a small river. Many toasts were drunk. The host, after drinking three bottles of Schloss Johanisburger, gave a hugh 'Hoch' and dashing his glass to the floor, swore that neither he nor his descendants would change a stone of the village. It would remain for ever unaltered, a memorial of a splendid day's sport; unequalled in the succeeding century when modern rifles replaced his out-dated weapons. A motheaten giant boar's head remains to this day gazing down at visitors as they enter the front door; beneath it a plaque records the details of the animals slaughtered on one of the happiest days of the Grand Duke's life.

The pretty state of Werthiem, after its forced absorption into Prussia, retained a measure of independence and even after the First World War and the declaration of a republic, the Grand Duke's former subjects continued to allow him the use of his name and title and the retention of his breweries, coal mines, iron works and factories. This ensured that although he had lost his sovereign powers he was far better off than his ancestors whose wealth a hundred years before had depended on the felling of trees.

The village remained untouched. A tannery and various small factories were rejected. The villagers, the elders resigned, the younger men discontented, continued to live behind the times. Their dull lives were enlivened only by a few memorable days in the autumn when the village reverted to paganism with the celebration of the cider harvest. Outbursts of the joy of living silenced criticism and shut the gossips' mouths. The inevitable result was pregnancies, put right by marriages and occasionally a tragedy, a cheap price to pay for a Bacchanal, when generosity reigned, and all but the poorest, who lived in the long tumbledown street at the western end of the village, filled and laid down their kegs. None were left out of the celebrations. The oldest derelicts could be seen walking unsteadily with pieces of bread and salted cheese to avert the annual attacks of colic caused by the constant filling of their mugs by unusually friendly neighbours.

August Schubler was born into this petrified community in 1919. His father had been killed in the trenches in the previous year. The boy did not suffer by his death; his mother, a large stern woman with red hair scraped into a bun, a formidable nose and little conversation, ran the house, paddock and orchard with determination which won her the reputation of 'a woman who could do without a husband'.

August grew up with twelve village boys in his school class. His life followed a repetitive pattern: he milked his mother's cow every morning, mowed the grass in the spring, first for his mother and then for neighbours with more land; swam, fished in the river in the hot summer evenings, attended the school and the Protestant church where the bearded pastor was an institution. Neither could he imagine the village without the bespectacled, hunchback doctor, a good man, regarded with awe, who always knocked on the door of his pregnant patients at the right moment. Once the Grand Duke, hearing of his powers, asked him up to the hunting lodge for an explanation. Smiling, he answered: 'I know the villagers well and when I see a girl's stomach swelling I just take a look at her and say to myself "12 o'clock, August 2nd" or "4 a.m., September 3rd". It is strange, I am always right. But it is a useless gift for they often say they were about to send for me anyway.'

August, not a bright pupil, learned to read and write with difficulty. He was caned for no particular reason no more or less than his contemporaries and took his beatings without a murmur, but shook his head on the way home, aware his mother would repeat the punishment. He was sure her arm was stronger than the schoolmaster's, but it never entered his head to conceal or complain. A thin, fair-haired boy who seldom smiled, he had companions rather than friends; but for the unusual length and strength of his arms, he would have been bullied.

At fourteen he started to work in the Grand Duke's woods; the foreman soon found he had gained a remarkable pupil. Before long foresters came from miles away to see him cross cut, down cut, with such accuracy that when the tree had fallen in precisely the right direction, so level was the stump that it looked as if it had been cut by a handsaw. His future seemed secure. The Grand Duke was on good terms with the Nazi regime which he considered had saved Germany. No changes disturbed the pattern of the little community's life.

In May 1939 August was drafted into the army. He was sad to miss the apple picking and cider making for the first time in his life. To his mother's annoyance he arranged that two of his contemporaries, whose parents' hay he had cut for the last four years, would help her out with the haymaking. She was outraged and sent them packing, saying: 'I can do the work myself.' But as they walked slowly away she called them back and told them her wrist was sprained but she would only accept their help on condition that they each took one eighth of the harvest. They demurred. She said 'that or nothing', and so it was.

August found army life difficult. He took a long time to understand the simple mechanism of his rifle. But he was far stronger than anyone else in his draft, and became a hero when a boy from his village boasted that his friend could cut down a pine tree in four minutes and fell it on a chosen spot. He was challenged and accepted. The event caused a stir beyond his regiment and many bets were laid as to whether or not he could succeed. What started as a village boast turned into a regimental drama and the Colonel, Count von Scheer, an owner of large woodlands, decided to watch. If the boy could do what he claimed, he would give him work. He could do with an expert tree feller. Such a forester would be a good investment.

On the day of the trial officers, non-commissioned officers and men watched in three interested groups. A measurer, starter and timekeeper had been chosen, but August paid little attention to the fuss – he had often been watched by curious admirers before – and waited patiently for the officer to fire his revolver. When the signal was given he worked swiftly and accurately round the tree. Soon the large pine was poised on a central column. With an effortless side cut he felled it between two standing trees. The task had taken exactly three and a half minutes. His backers had won. That night he was offered beer in the sergeants', wine in the officers', mess, Count von Scheer took him aside and said he would make him his head forester when his service was completed. August was surprised and replied, 'My family have worked for the Grand Duke's ancestors and lived in the same house for two hundred years; it would kill my mother to move, I cannot leave her.' The Count said no more; he did not wish to offend the Grand Duke but, noticing August was scrupulously clean, punctual and sober, decided he would make a good batman.

When war broke out in September 1939 the two men had established a perfect understanding. August never forgot an order, and lived up to the Colonel's optimistic hopes by seeing he never ran out of soap, new tooth-brushes and razor blades. Each day he carefully washed an ivory handled, badger hair shaving brush with a herb lotion his mother sent him from the forest; she had used it on her father and husband's brushes. This delighted the Colonel and every morning as he stroked the silky hairs he congratulated himself on selecting August. Both were big men, standing six foot two. There the resemblance ended. The aristocratic Colonel had black hair, brushed smoothly back over a flat head, a thin, clean-shaven face, hooked nose, black eyes, a slit of a mouth, and a chin jutting forward to a sharp point. The army was his life. Still in his late thirties it was expected that he would rise to a high rank. An observant martinet, he never missed the slightest errors of his officers and men, but he was fair and praised excellence; as a result his regiment was one of the most efficient in the Reich. Although not popular he was respected and feared. August had blond cropped hair, blue eyes, a straight nose and a mouth which hung a little open. His chin was slightly inverted; despite his muscular body he resembled a giant rabbit. When he had nothing to do he would sit still, his eyes open, thinking. If he was asked what about, he would say, 'Home, I suppose'. When he came out of his reveries he had few memories, except that they were about his life in the village. In the regiment, he was not envied, unlike those who took advantage of their officers, neither was he admired. A quiet young man without friends or enemies he went seriously and soberly about his duties. He had never slept with a girl but when he woke up in the morning he often felt twinges of desire. Two years before his mother had told him he was too good-natured to choose a wife and would, if left to himself, be taken in by some hussy, 'who will make a fool of you'. Occasionally he dreamed of a big fair girl with a strong firm body but was willing to wait for his mother to produce her. He often thought how pleasant it would be to come home and sit by his own fireside with his mother and wife.

On the outbreak of war in 1939 his regiment was one of the first to move into Poland: when the weight of German armour broke through the Polish lines, Von Scheer's regiment was given the duty of mopping up the survivors. This entailed searching the countryside. Every evening August heard comic stories of the time Poles took to drown, and how a sergeant had found, by the blood on the end of his bayonet, three Poles in a haystack – how, when he burnt it down, the farmer and his wife cried with rage and beat the charred bodies, cursing them as now they would have no fodder for the winter. August sympathised with the farmer. He remembered the care with which his mother had made their own haystack in the paddock and that on every fine early summer evening she would walk into the woods and carry home a bundle of grass while he, a little boy – with a few wisps in each hand – trotted behind. Once a hard winter had been followed by a wet haymaking season and their cow was hungry by July, causing his mother to buy fodder at a price which made her click her tongue and shake her head for months. As for the Poles, they were enemies. When he joined the army he learned that Germany was surrounded by hatred and Czechoslovakia, Poland, France, England and all Jews wished to destroy Germany, burn down the Black Forest and misrule the country again as they had after 1918. He had not realised these things or that without the Führer, the enemies of the Reich would have enslaved the Fatherland. His sergeant told him Germany was ruled by a great man and explained how the English and French had made the Reichmark worthless so you could neither buy or sell and that thousands of Germans had died of starvation. As it was, he was fortunate to serve in the German army in Poland. This lecture made August feel patriotic and he cried when the Führer talked to him on the wireless.

As a batman he had few duties but looked after his Colonel carefully and was worried when he stayed up late at night talking to his officers, reading official documents and drafting orders. One of August's tasks was to bring his master a cup of hot chocolate as a nightcap. To begin with in peace-time he had made it whenever the Colonel went to bed, but on active service he was given orders to place a thermos by his bedside. He noticed the Colonel always drunk every drop; it must have helped him to sleep. One morning August tasted a spilt teaspoonful in the saucer and was shocked to find it tasted stale.

That night he positioned his bed in the commandeered Polish barracks so that he could see across a courtyard into the bedroom where his officer sat working at his desk. He lay back and woke himself up by an alarm clock every quarter of an hour, until at three o'clock he saw the Colonel stand up and stretch himself. August at once ran downstairs, dashed past the guard into the officers' quarters, mixed fresh chocolate and milk before walking loudly upstairs. The Colonel, who was undressing, turned round with an angry look, August wondered if it was because he had missed his chocolate, but when he saw the tray his eyes softened, he said nothing.

Every night until they moved forward again, August followed the same procedure. Their next base was a half-ruined village and when he was unpacking the Colonel said, 'Now, there is to be no nonsense about waiting up watching me; put a thermos by my bed and go to sleep yourself. That is an order, understand?'

The loyal batman heard affection in the tones of the usually curt voice, and swore to himself that he would die for this man.

Afterwards, the Colonel was promoted and became a Major General in the 1942 campaign in Russia. August never forgot the terrible cold of that winter. But he always thought of his master and would, every day, find fuel even if he had to cut down wooden outbuildings with his axe to the fury of the owners.

In late November 1942 the General was in command of a division attempting to relieve the surrounded Germany garrison in Stalingrad. August listened to a special message broadcast by the Führer which told the advancing army to beware of the treacherous Russians. All those captured should be shot. He began to worry that as a non-combatant, he had never killed an enemy of the Reich. He dwelt on the matter, finally plucked up his courage and asked if he could, while remaining a batman, join the squad which daily shot enemy spies. The General looked surprised and asked, 'Why?'

'Because the Führer says it is the duty of all German soldiers to kill the enemies of the Reich and I have not done so.' The General looked at him before answering in a toneless voice, 'You are right, it is your duty to follow the commands of the Führer, and if you wish to interpret them in this way I grant your request.'

The style of the executions depended on the squad

captains. The humanitarians took a pistol and finished off the wounded. Others, having made sure the victims would not recover, left them alive on the ground. One execution stuck in August's mind; his squad had aimed at eighteen Russians with orders to fire three volleys. When the firing was over two of the men continued to move. August looked at them with interest. They could not crawl but made gurgling noises, and groped with their hands, blood seeping out of the corners of their mouths. Suddenly to his surprise he saw two of his companions firing, without permission, at the heads. The officer placed them under arrest, and turning to the remainder, some of whom were standing unsteadily with legs apart, ordered them never to waste bullets; adding that if he had his way Russian prisoners would be used for realistic bayonet practice to toughen up recruits, accustom them to killing and save ammunition which one day might be needed. August later thought the matter over and nodded his head. His mother had brought him up to avoid waste.

At the end of December the German relief force were only thirty miles from Stalingrad. The belief was that the besieged army would break out and join their saviours in a pincer movement. The Führer forbade this opportunity as 'unworthy of German honour'. The batman noticed that the decision made his General edgier than usual, and from then on took two blue and red pills each night. Early one morning August (after a perfunctory knock) walked into the cement underground quarters where the General had his office. A green light showed he was alone. His master lay slumped forward, his arms spread-eagled over a makeshift desk. August waited without moving or speaking until to his relief the General slowly raised his head and forced himself upright in his chair. Slowly his expression changed and his eyelids drooped. 'Do you know the position?' he said. 'If General Paulos broke out we could join up with him and all retreat in good order to Kotelnikovski. But he's not allowed to. Can you tell me why?' he added in a questioning voice which did not expect an answer.

August said nothing.

'I am not a weak man,' the General went on, getting up and walking up and down, 'but I cannot see the point of waste, not only of men, but of tanks, guns, ammunition. I cannot understand it.'

He sat down again, shook his head and said in a tired voice August had never heard before, 'You know, you must be quiet about what I have said. Remember, as I do, it is a soldier's duty to obey.'

He leaned forward, put his elbows on the table, his face in his hands. His behaviour worried his batman who could not understand why, if the Führer ordered General Paulos to remain in Stalingrad, it was not his duty to remain. He puzzled for a long time over the matter, without finding an answer.

He noticed after the surrender of the German garrison his General changed. Before he had always worked with intense efficiency. Now he looked tired and one day August heard an old friend, still a colonel, saying to him, 'You cannot try to know all your officers, visit every section under your command, interview people morning, afternoon, evening until you are grey in the face with fatigue, be called at six, read and write papers all day and night without paying a price. You must relax or collapse.'

August wondered why his master was so depressed. Stalingrad was only a temporary setback. After all, the Germans were the master race and would win the war despite a temporary reversal. He had only to compare himself to the captives to see the difference between the two nations.

The German army retreated and in June 1943 he saw

his General upset again. He told August in an expression-less voice that he was going to leave his division and become an inspector of prison camps. He would be taking up his new post within a month, his batman would be coming with him. August was messing in a green tent under pine trees. He often heard his fellow batmen discussing the necessity of wiping out the Jews who were polluting ther pure German races. Nearly every man in the room had a story to tell of how a Jew had swindled their friends and forced them to sell their farms and shops in order to pay ruinous interest. August had no such memory; all he could remember was an old Jewish pedlar who came every year to the village with a wooden box, divided into four drawers, tied on his back. Boys gazed at resilvered pocket knives, coloured whistles, spikes to prise stones out of horses' hooves, bright bootlaces and so on. Old Isaac always started his round in the upper part of the village where the rich timber merchants lived. He then descended to the tradesmen's houses where another drawer was produced. After meeting a crowd of children by the timber yard, he would end his tour in the poor area by the river with a drawerful of glittering knick-knacks. The whole village looked forward to the visits and August was surprised to learn of the villainy of his race and horrified to hear that they used Christian babies as religious sacrifices. If this was the case it was right to eliminate them. A staff major's batman always raised a laugh whenever he repeated his favourite joke: 'The best smell I have ever known in my life was when I passed through Treblinka. You can smell burning Jews.' Whenever he said this another batman always added, 'No man with a weak nose should ever visit that town.' Their companions always smiled and nodded their heads.

At the end of April August was given two weeks' leave which, excluding travelling, meant ten days at home. On his return to the village he thought at first it had hardly changed. His mother looked older but the schoolmaster, the doctor and the pastor had not aged. However, when he walked down to the lower village he saw, to his surprise, wounded soldiers sitting on doorsteps. Two long, low, wooden buildings had sprung up on the slope behind the street, against the wishes of the Grand Duke, who felt his ancestors had been betrayed. One of the buildings was for wounded men, the other for the permanently disabled. August's mother explained that meant those who would never walk again. Military rejects and even the deformed had all been called away to work in factories; only old men and women remained to sweep, clean, carry wood and look after patients.

On his second day at home August was bored with doing nothing and went round his mother's orchard pruning (although it was too late in the year). He was dismayed to see the tangled groups in the centres of the apple trees which would prevent the sun from ripening the young fruit. He also cut down sycamore saplings which had sprung up during the three years he had been away, and would soon overshadow the mature apple trees.

He was sitting contented after the midday meal when his mother said 'I have been careful for your sake, and used my own mother's money to live on and never touched your father's savings which now amount to a tidy little sum. Your family were always close, without smoking, drinking or wasteful ways. Now that you are rising twenty-five, it is time you married. I have been looking for a local girl who would suit you when this cursed war is over. Do you know Farmer Hegel's place?'

August nodded, suddenly excited, remembering his thoughts in the cold Russian nights of the warm arms of a strong young wife.

'Well, their niece, Anna, lives there now. Six months

ago she came out of the town to milk the cows. Both her cousins have been killed. The old people are going to leave her the farm. She is twenty-one and I hear fancies you. Perhaps you are slyer than I thought,' she added, looking carefully at her son, before continuing: 'This evening at seven o'clock you are to walk up through the woods until you reach the tip stone, then take the path to the right towards the valley where the farm lies, stop after fifty yards at a huge oak standing at a cross path. She will pass that way soon bringing her cows down the hill, home. You are not to be shy, but shake hands; if you like her, take out your handkerchief when you say goodbye. I know you are too bashful to do more. But look your best.'

August was amazed to hear a girl he had never heard of liked him. How could she? As he walked up the hill in the morning he felt his heart beating with excitement and imagined a wife in his warm bed. He lingered on the crosspath by an oak tree. Nobody appeared. Had his mother got it wrong and the girl was not coming? Had he got the wrong place? He began to tremble with disappointment. At last he almost jumped for joy: he had heard the sound of bells. Soon a herd of thirty cows came into sight, jostling their calves. They were followed by a tall, slim girl wearing a long green skirt below a short-sleeved white blouse. When August saw her shining eyes, brown arms and smiling face he felt like running away. She did not seem to notice his terror, walked up to him, gave a little curtsey and said, 'I am Anna,' and looked into his eyes. Her calmness made him so confused he was not sure later what colour her eyes were. She lifted her hand, shook her head and two long chestnut pigtails fell down her back.

'What a shy fellow you are,' she said. 'Why don't you look at me? I have seen you before although you never gave me a glance.'

He stared at her. She smiled. 'You were too busy cutting

a tree down. We had come up from our town for a week
and my uncle took us up to see you; I was not looking
forward to it. But when I saw you cutting the tree, I liked
you. I could not get over the movement of your arms. I
was hoping I would see you again and then your aunt
came to talk about money, which my uncle cannot resist.
I could not believe it, I was so happy. Now we have met
at last!'

August had never dreamed he would hear such words
spoken in a laughing voice, untouched by embarrassment.
She put her hands around his right arm and said his
muscles felt good. Then she told him to sit down by her
on the short grass and asked if he was disappointed.
August, tongue-tied, answered, 'Yes', at which this strange
girl threw herself back on the grass. He felt desperate;
everything had gone wrong; he tried hard to remember his
mother's instructions. With a sudden movement he pulled
out his handkerchief. She burst out laughing.

'You are a funny boy, shy as your mother said. But
come tomorrow and every day until your leave's up,
except Saturday, when some lads from the factory are
coming up with their girls and we are having a party in a
pine grove and will sing and dance: you would not enjoy
that. Now, my intended, say farewell to your future wife
with a kiss. Or at least show me your handkerchief again.'

August knew he did not know how to kiss her and,
miserable, put his hand on his handkerchief at which Anna
– she had become to him a beautiful, unreal, blurred
apparition – put her hand to her mouth and turned away.
Hurt, he started to walk home but had not gone far when
she ran up, turned him round, took him in her arms and
pulling his head down on her shoulders, pressed her cheeks
against his. He had never known such a wonderful feeling
and when she kissed his cheek he thought he would faint.
She reached round his back and pulled him to her and for

the first time in his life he felt a woman's breasts pressing against him. He felt giddy and the next thing he knew was that he was lying on the grass holding his handkerchief. From the bottom of the hill came the sound of bells. Dazed, cursing his cowardliness, he walked home.

When he arrived back his mother was digging in the garden; without looking up she asked, 'Did you take your handkerchief out?'

'Yes,' he said sheepishly. She neither replied or stopped digging. He was relieved.

August woke up next morning in his attic, facing east. He had never been allowed curtains, and only shutters in winter, to allow the sun to wake him up early for school. He immediately knew his life had changed. He was in love with a girl whose blurred face he could not remember. But he could remember her breasts pushing against him. He shut his eyes and raised his arms pretending to hold her to him. How could he win her, show that he was not altogether stupid? He looked at his diary, although he knew the exact dates by heart, to reassure himself it was Wednesday which meant that, excluding the Saturday when she was seeing her friends – he was glad she had not asked him to meet them, he would have cut such a poor figure – eight days of his leave remained. He tried hard to think of ways to please her, in vain. He was frightened. Anna was laughing at him, her marriage proposal nothing but a joke. He took out his axe and chopped the saplings into logs, his mind wandered. He slept badly. At breakfast he looked down at his plate and asked his mother what he could do to win Anna. She looked at him, shook her head, twisted her mouth into a smile, stood up and locked herself in the scullery where, August knew, she had a secret hiding place. She returned in a few minutes with four boxes which she put on the table and slowly unpacked. Her son watched in amazement. Looking unusually pleased, she told him that when old Isaac had come on his rounds for the last time in 1939, she had taken four gifts off him, two of them were to be returned the next year. 'But he never came again and never will. I keep them in case he does. He left them with me,' she said, 'because I had been his customer for twenty years and always paid his price without questioning. He said he trusted me and nobody else. He was wrong, for I had always sold what I bought from him, for a good profit, even if I had to wait for years. But I have kept these gifts for you, I told him I would and he gave me good advice.'

August paid no attention to her words but watched, fascinated as she laid out in turn a silver wrist watch, a charm bracelet, a sparkling purple ring and a little golden watch swinging on a chain.

'Now,' said his mother, pushing them forward, 'I explained to him that one day you would marry. Isaac knew about girls, but of course not about this one as they never met. He said they all love presents. I never cared for them myself, but he said it is as if "they are flying their lover's flag and want the world to know". He said there are two types of girls, the practical, who go for good value, and the giddy, who like showy things. Now Anna seems to me to be a practical girl, but you never can tell. So you are to take all four up this evening and let her choose two of them. Isaac said, "Tell him not to say a word about my choosing them or it will take half her pleasure away." If she asks you where they are from, act canny and say you travelled to find them. "Mystery," Isaac said, "pleases a girl".'

That evening August felt self-conscious and uneasy as he walked up to the tipping stone. For the first time he was carrying a basket with a pink ribbon on the handle. He was glad no-one had seen him. When he reached their trysting place he sat down on the grass and had an idea,

74

which pleased him immensely. He laid the four boxes on a flat stretch of grass, and sat and waited. At last he heard distant bells and then muffled shuffling, followed by the cows pushing against each other as they walked down the path. Anna walked behind them with a red handkerchief on her hair, wearing again a white blouse, above a bright blue skirt. She shouted something to her charges who paused for a moment and then slowly moved on. Leaving them she climbed up the bank towards him whistling a tune.

'Well, you're here,' she said, 'I knew you would be. I am glad all the same.' She saw the boxes, stood still and gazed at them with intense interest, unaware of August. This gave him the courage to stare at her for the first time. He saw beneath her handkerchief dark brown curls falling over her forehead above brown eyes with black eyelashes, brown red cheeks, full red lips over a rounded chin. August was so busy looking at her he never thought of saying anything. At last Anna turned to him and said seriously, 'Well, you are a surprise. I never knew you were a pedlar. Have you come to sell me something?' He jumped with dismay.

His surprise made her laugh and sit down by him, hiding the boxes. Their concealment threw August into complete confusion. Was she going to ignore his gifts?

'Well!' she said at last as he sat silent, red with embarrassment, 'may I examine your stock?'

'Choose,' he blurted out, his face a fiery red.

She turned sideways and picking up one of the boxes, slowly and carefully untied the red ribbon, folded it, put it on her knee, before treating the wrapping in the same way. When she opened the box and saw the silver chain with three charms, a cathedral, a heart, a lamb, she moved quickly. In a second it was on her wrist, which she was holding up and turning around. She gazed at it in silence, her face serious. At last she put it back in its box, meticulously replaced the paper and ribbon and put it carefully down. Then with the same care she unpacked the second parcel, examined the silver wrist watch, turned to him quickly, put her hand out, gripped his thumb, said in an uneven voice: 'You set it at the right time.'

August flushed even redder. The girl did not notice; her eyes had resettled on her wrist. At last reluctantly she put it away, opened the third packet, the hanging watch. She gave it a careless glance, swung it to and fro and said, looking him straight in the face, 'It's not for me – what would I want with a pretty thing like this swinging about up here? It would only fall off. What is the good of a present if you lose it?'

The last box contained a ring. Anna lifted it up, turned it to catch the light, stared hard and said slowly, 'You know it is an amethyst.' August shook his head; he had no idea.

'I have always loved amethysts.' She held it up, unable to stop looking at it. At last she put it on the third finger of her left hand and, unpacking the second box again, put the silver watch on her right wrist. She lay back, lifted her hands and turned them about with such graceful movements that August held his breath.

Eventually, Anna packed all the little boxes into the basket, put her hands between her knees, looked at August tenderly and patted the grass next to her. When he had nervously moved over she put her head on his shoulder, stroked his hair and said, 'You must have got up early and taken a lot of trouble to please me; you could not have found such things in the village. The pedlar has not come since the war.' She moved her head away and gripped his left hand in her fingers. His joy was so intense he did not dare to move. She told him his hand felt like a dead fish. He squeezed her so hard she wrung her fingers and put her hands on her knees. Then she looked at him and said, 'As we are going to be married and I know all about you and your family – you are a famous man around here you know – I will tell you about myself. I was brought up in our town and had a happy childhood, except at home, in fact I have never been really unhappy so I hope you will not be unkind to me. When I was sixteen and had finished school I went into the factory which makes rifle bullets. Hundreds of cases would come along in rows and I pressed a button and powder fell into them. Oh, it was hard to bear. I made many friends in the summer and we went out every Sunday into the country for picnics. I will tell you I have liked three boys, that's all. I know I am modern in telling you all this but I want to be honest with you. I don't know why.'

She bent down and kissed his thumb. 'Then my father's and mother's health started failing. He was gassed in the first war. Anyway, for years they were more interested in God than me. You know sometimes in the forest I believe in God, not the town god who is only believed in on Sundays. When my parents died I was sad, not unhappy. You see how honest I am. Well, when my cousins were killed and I was asked to come here I was pleased to leave all those bullets and came, though I feared it might be dull. It was not. I thought you would come back one day – I never forgot you. I have a way with animals and the cows soon became fond of me. Friends come up every weekend and sometimes in the week time and sit and talk about what we will do when the war is over. I have a little hut up higher; I can sit in it and read. But I am pleased you have come for me. I knew one day you would. I am sorry about Saturday but you would hate it. I cannot see you dancing and singing.'

She laughed again; he had never met anybody who laughed so much. His mother never laughed.

'Anyhow,' Anna said, 'I am going to be practical, as I can't make up my mind between the silver chain with charms, the ring and the wrist watch. I am going to take them home tonight and tell you my choice tomorrow, if you trust me, that is. I am going to take the hanging watch as well, although I don't want it. But I like the idea of putting the four parcels on my bed and pretending I have not opened them.'

He tried to get up, but instead kicked her hard on the ankle. She cried out but said with a smile, 'Well, as I like your strength, I will have to put up with your clumsiness.'

She put her hands round his neck, kissed him on the mouth, pressed against him, said he was not to move or he would hurt her again, stood up, looked down on him, smiled, gently stroked his face, glanced at her old gun metal watch and said, 'I must be going home or the cows will be there before me and start mooing and then my aunt will think I am dead and start crying.'

She smiled 'goodbye', and with a wave ran quickly down the hill. August thought she floated, now and again flying over a stone or rut. He watched her with intense concentration, and gazed for a long time at a large bush behind which she finally disappeared.

They met again on Friday. August still could not control his nerves. And when Anna ran up to him he remained unbending, leaned back and said good morning. 'Oh my, my,' she said, 'you're as stiff as a ramrod. Now I am going to soften you up. Come, we will find a comfortable seat.'

When they sat down she put her arm firmly through his, showed him the silver watch on her wrist and grasped his large thumb, saying it was nearly as big as her hand.

'You did not mind my telling you the truth, did you?' she said and added, 'That's what God tells us to do, isn't it?' He didn't know what he thought, but nodded.

'Now it's your turn,' she said, looking at him seriously. 'Tell me about yourself and your girls.'

'I haven't had any.'

'What?' she said. 'None? Never walked out with a girl?'

'Never.' She paused and said doubtfully, 'You like girls, don't you?' He said solemnly: 'I love you', and looked at her so innocently that she flung her arms around his neck.

'Oh, I do fancy you,' she said. 'But you are odd; have you really never danced or kissed anybody?' He shook his head.

'Why?'

'Well, my mother said she'd find me a wife . . .'

'Well, it's lucky she found me, isn't it? What if she had produced some cross-eyed hunchback? Would you have married her?' He did not know but answered, 'No, not if I had seen you. I would never marry or love anyone but you. I know that will always be so.'

The tenderness in his voice made her cry and she put her head in his lap, forcing him to make the first positive act of courtship of his life, a rough stroking of her hair. She looked up at him and said, 'I am going to show you how to kiss me.' When she put her tongue in his mouth he jerked away and she had to pull him by his hair towards her. They lay side by side on the grass, clinging to each other. Her life had not been as easy and simple as she had made out. Her father and mother were cold, unaffectionate church-goers. She had been overworked in the factory and sometimes bored up in the grasslands. But she had always made the best of things and enjoyed herself, determined one day to marry and have children. Would she have married another man to have a family? She did not know or care. Now this strange, huge, strong innocent who had always been at the back of her mind was to be her husband. He made her feel secure and happy. As for August, he felt she made up for all the starkness of his youth, the kisses his mother had never given him, her beatings and crossness. He rested his head on her bosom. He had never experienced kindness and thought he was the luckiest man in the world. When they said goodbye she thrust the three parcels into his hand, saying quickly, 'I have chosen the silver wrist watch, not the ring. It will be more useful.'

August hit his forehead and cried out in an angry voice, 'You make me forget everything. I . . . I . . . meant you to have two things.'

Her eyes opened. 'Oh, I am so happy, so happy. I loved the useless ring much the best, but the watch was useful and pretty.' To his alarm tears came into her eyes. 'You know,' she said, giving him a puzzled glance, 'it was a clever trick of yours to say I could only have one; it made me love the ring more when I thought I could not have it.' She sat down, opened the parcel, stared at the ring, put it on her finger, wiped her eyes and ran down the hill. August as usual walked home confused.

The next day seven of Anna's friends arrived at the farm bringing a large picnic basket and bottles of hock in wet straw. They climbed the hill, lunched beneath a group of trees, drank, jigged, sang songs, drank again, slept until evening, walked down the hill, singing, to the farm. Anna flirted with two of her old admirers. They said they had never seen her looking prettier. She had to push them away.

August, on the other hand, went up to the grand ducal lodge and asked the head gardener who lived in the lodge, 'Do any trees need felling?' 'Yes, two pines in the garden.' The man added, 'The Grand Duke said this year there is not a man in all Germany except August who can fell them without damaging my bushes.' They went and examined the site carefully. August thought the Grand Duke was right: he would have to be very careful. He was;

only one azalea branch was snapped. Then August cut off the branches of the firs, dragged them out of the garden and made a bonfire. As he was bending down to pile the hot ashes together a voice said: 'Ah, I had been waiting for you.'

August looked up and was amazed to see the Grand Duke, who went on, 'I knew you were the only man who could do it. I thought the whole azalea clump would be crushed but you have only snapped off a small branch. Well done.'

The old man put his hand in his pocket, took out two gold coins and gave them to August. He seemed to have shrunk and looked older. Had he always been so small? In the past he had seemed so important that August had hardly dared look at him. Now he saw a little old man with drooping moustaches and grey hair, leaning on a silver-handled stick. The Grand Duke called for beer. A large tankard appeared on a silver tray. August was made to sit down on a wooden seat, a thing he had never dreamed could happen. He was asked about the war and found himself repeating the exact words his General had used at Stalingrad.

The Grand Duke stood up and walked up and down in the same way as the General had done; afterwards he did not ask any more questions and, looking smaller than ever, walked away leaving August to finish his drink alone.

On Sunday the lovers met again. August marvelled at Anna's beauty and gracefulness, but noticed she was avoiding him and would pick a flower or edge away if he tried to touch her. She made up for her coldness by allowing him to walk her back to the farm hand in hand. He remembered not to crush her fingers too hard but had no inkling that although she had decided to give herself to him she wished to prolong their courting. On Monday she was friendly, kind, but distant; disappointed, he loved her more than ever.

The evening before his last day she told him to meet her higher up the hill at midday but he was not to bring any food. She was going to show him what a good housewife she would be. When he arrived he saw a snow-white tablecloth spread out under a chestnut tree. He had never been to a picnic and was amazed when he saw an open wine bottle, two glasses, fresh white bread, butter, a cream cheese, two other cheeses, hard-boiled eggs, lettuces and a chicken cut into four parts. He feared a friend was coming to join them. A folded cloak lay against the tree. They sat together against the chestnut bole and he ate all the bread and butter and chicken and nearly all the cheeses. She kept smiling and filling up his wine glass but only ate an egg, and a little cheese and lettuce.

When they had finished he lay back lazily (she had told him not to move while she packed up the picnic). When she had finished, he admired her deft efficiency. She smiled at him, picked up the cloak, walked round the tree, found a patch of grass dappled with sunshine, laid it down, said with a little shiver she could not bear spiders running up her back, and began to undress. When she saw him gazing at her in astonishment she told him to do the same. He tried to turn his back but she told him to turn round. 'I want always to remember everything about this day, do not be silly.'

Excited by the wine, his face red with embarrassment, he undid his boots, took off his socks and trousers and shirt. When he had finished undressing she was lying naked. He noticed how white her body was compared to her arms, neck and face. She beckoned to him. When he made love to her she shut her eyes and remembered her first sight of his majestic heaving arm muscles as he cut down the trees. She dug her fingers into his back. It was all too much for him; he thought he was dreaming and after he had loved her he collapsed into a state of amazed contentment.

They lay together all the afternoon; for once she did not bother about the herd. He made love to her again and they slept and were woken by the cows mooing as if to say it was time they were milked. He dressed without embarrassment, and on the way down she sang to him songs of faithful love, but made him stop before they came to the farm, saying as she stroked his arm, 'Go home now, if they see you my aunt will be sure to say something silly. I don't want our day spoilt. You know now I belong to you and you to me. One day we will live in the farm and have children.'

She put her arms gently around his neck, hugged him quickly and ran away.

When he reached home his mother told him to turn around as he started to walk upstairs. She said nothing but gave a small, satisfied smile. The next day she said goodbye without kissing him. He gave her the Grand Duke's two gold pieces and asked her to send them to Anna. In the night he had decided it was time she started to prepare her trousseau. His mother nodded without smiling. He was relieved she asked no questions.

He caught a train to Crakow. He had no idea where it was but, obeying orders, gave notes to separate station masters signed by the General and counterstamped by Himmler's office. To his surprise he was treated with unusual respect; the station masters went out of their way to help him. Twice, to his dismay, he was put in reserved first class carriages. The journey took longer than expected due to the disruption of the railway lines. When August arrived, he found his CO billeted in a hotel, tired but pleased to see him. Later in the evening the General, in an embarrassed voice, told him things were going badly. 'As

Leningrad remains unconquered our lines are stretched and communications complicated by the endless forests in which partisans train and destroy vehicles. We are told to shoot not the prisoners but Russians. They still blow up the railway lines and are stopping supplies urgently needed at the front.' August wondered why his master was giving such a detailed explanation and at the same time looking fixedly at him. The General continued: 'You know, it has always been the policy of the Führer to kill off the Jews both in Germany and the new lands, including Poland, where they breed like rabbits. He has created camps to obliterate the race. It is no easy task. There are millions of them. You cannot make men evaporate; they have not only to be killed but buried. This sounds no problem but it is. The earth throws up the dead. Also these Jews rebel, escape, join the Russians in the forests. I have been given the job of stopping these escapes. Last week I went to four camps: Auschwitz, Sobibor, Majdanek and Belzec. That was enough to make me understand why prisoners, faced with death, risk everything to get away. It is my duty to prevent them. When I arrived at Sobibor yesterday I found they had arrested a Dutchman who had plotted, with the Ukranians, a breakout of several hundred Jews. The obstinate fool had been interrogated to make him give us names but he remains obdurate. It is necessary he should name those that helped him; in the camp are approximately seventy of his countrymen of all ages. After I learned interrogation had failed, I gave orders that if he would talk he would save all his countrymen's lives.'

August noticed the General was no longer looking him in the eyes but was staring at his blotter, talking slowly in an expressionless voice. 'He has remained silent, seventy men, women and children will be beheaded tomorrow morning. The executions will stop immediately he speaks. My orders,' the General added, looking up, 'have come from above. I asked the Sobibor HQ if they could efficiently carry out a mass decapitation. They said yes, but it is usually a messy business and heads are often only severed after two or three blows! I thought of you. Are you prepared to behead seventy Dutchmen, women and children tomorrow? Yes or no? All I will say is if you can face it, you will prevent unnecessary suffering.'

August, thinking of Anna, heard the General as though he was speaking through a mist but saw he was worried. He wished to help him and the Führer for he knew how both the Dutch and the Jews had for years plotted to overthrow the Reich. He saluted.

'Sir, I will do my duty. What time do I start?' To his surprise the General pursed his lips. But all he said was, 'Thank you, have you no qualms?'

'No. I will see they do not suffer.'

Afterwards he wondered if Anna had softened his character. He could only think of her. The General still stared at him. Was he afraid his batman would let him down? To reassure him August said he was anxious to carry out orders. The expression on the General's face did not change.

Next morning he was driven to Sobibor and arrived at Camp 3 at six-thirty. The staff car pulled up on one side of a rough, untarmacced square surrounded by huts. Search lights lit up the area. He picked out two groups of men with between them an elongated block of wood against which leaned, he was proudly told by a corporal, the eighteenth century executioner's axe from Lodz.

The smallest group consisted of four people, a drooping man propped up with difficulty by two German soldiers: his nose was swollen and had moved towards his right cheek bone; bloody foam bubbled out of the corners of his mouth. One of his arms hung limp, his clothes looked stiff. By him was a sergeant major holding a thin whip with which, now and again, he lashed the prisoner on the face, his broken arm or the few bloodless spots on his clothes, saying each time in a toneless voice, 'Name the conspirators and you will save your countrymen's lives.'

The prisoner never replied except to feebly shake his head, spattering his guards with spots of blood. They were changed every half hour. At eight o'clock the first Dutchman, or rather boy – he looked about ten – was led out of the larger group, his neck placed on the block, his chin pushed over the end. A woman wailed and was hit in the mouth. An iron clamp was fixed over the thin little body so it could only give feeble kicks. After August had examined the axe and satisfied himself it was razor sharp, he took his coat off, gave an easy swing and lopped off the head. The sixth head belonged to a young woman; after she had been strapped down he noticed her long black hair. He asked why it had not been cropped and was told the Dutch group had only just arrived. The hair distracted him; he was afraid a gust of wind might obscure the correct cutting place. He always hated untidiness and asked for shears. After a short delay they were produced. He cut the woman's hair without hurting her head and was able to complete his work neatly. Later he was glad he had asked for them; two men, five women and seven little boys and girls needed hair cuts.

After August had cut off fifteen heads the work began to bore him. He did not like the sound of women and children's screams. They pierced his ears and made complete concentration difficult. He wished the Dutch were as silent as trees but then he remembered that he had soon tired of endless felling and had made it more interesting by carefully examining the health of the timber and the age rings in the wood. He started to examine the heads. One woman had two large moles, one on either side of her neck. He moved the angle of his legs and was pleased when the clean cut head fell to the ground. To his delight his axe had fallen exactly where he had planned, one mole had fallen with the head, the other remained visible on the neck, a quarter of an inch below the severance line. Another time he sliced exactly through the centre of a boil. Such problems revitalised him; he made no mistakes. Time passed quickly.

The last head belonged to the obstinate Dutchman. He never moved and August decided he was dead, but took careful aim. He did not wish to mar his record.

When the job was finished August felt satisfied. He fingered the axe's blade admiringly; it was as sharp as ever. He sadly reflected they did not make steel like that today and wished he could keep the wonderful piece of craftsmanship. He was thanked, an envelope placed in his hand, and returned by car to Crakow.

He slept nearly all the way, his journey had begun at three o'clock that morning. When he woke up he felt unusual and after a time realised it was the bulky envelope in his side pocket. He opened it. It was full of Reich marks, more than he could believe. Tears came into his eyes. He would send it home to Anna and tell her to buy a marriage bed. His mother had told him when they married she would move out of the best room and take her furniture with her.

During the next year the Russians advanced, the Germans withdrew. Despite this setback, the defeat in North Africa, the landings in Sicily, the retreats in Italy and France, it never entered August's head that Germany would not ultimately triumph. He noticed the General grow older and greyer. One evening in March 1945 he called for August and told him to sit down.

Leaning forward, his skin grey, his eyes dull he said: 'I am an old-fashioned German soldier, my father was in the army and his father was an officer in Bismarck's army which took Paris. I was always brought up to understand that an officer has a special relationship with his batman. I hope I have treated you justly; you have certainly served me loyally. I will not praise you for doing your duty, but I have not forgotten it. I think I have twice spoken to you in an irregular manner. I trusted you; I wished to talk. I was not wrong. The time has come to tell you the war is nearly over. I have done things which I had not expected to do. You have done more unpleasant things without complaint but you are a simple character. I am not trying to evade responsibility when I say it was easier for you to behead Jews than it was for me to ask you to do so. We are about to be defeated. The Americans and English are advancing from the west, the Russians from the east. Neither will have mercy on us. Today I order you to go by train to Prague. Here is your ticket. There you will join an office connected with the distribution of Red Cross parcels. Yesterday a man called Frederich Frott was killed here. You will take his name and passport. Do not fear anyone will mention your impersonation when you arrive. Much is going on today to prepare us to fight again, but not by me. Before I give you Frott's papers and some black dye, with which you are to change your appearance – but not until you enter the train – I wish to ask you one question. Do you feel guilty? Have I ever ordered you to carry out any action against your will? Think carefully.'

'No,' said August, 'I have always tried to do my duty to you and to the Führer.'

'That is what I thought. Here are your papers.' He held them out and said in a cold voice, 'Goodbye. You have served me faithfully according to your own standards. Good luck.'

For the first time since he had joined the army August felt like crying. He worshipped the General and now the tone of the voice of the man he loved was full of dislike.

What had he ever done but serve and obey? He felt bitterly hurt at such unkindness, saluted and quickly turned round. He did not wish the General to despise his unmanly grief.

The next day August squeezed into a train to Prague. When the Russian advance turned into a rout he was caught up in the universal confusion, pushed westward, arrested by the Americans and interrogated. He showed his papers, was locked up in prison for the night and released the next day. Finally he made his way back to Werthiem. A year later he heard, to his surprise and sorrow, that his General had shot himself.

Anna was happy to see him. She now owned the farm. They later sold it and moved into his mother's house. Today he has retired. The village has become a small town, his wife a local councillor. She leads a busy life and is a handsome, slim, laughing, brown woman, looking much younger than her age. She never questioned her husband about his war time activities. He would have told her everything. She was a strict but loving mother of six children, five boys and a girl. They have eighteen grand-children. August still loves her passionately. She only allows him to make love to her twice a week and no longer trembles when she feels his muscular arms. They are regarded as a happy couple and are respected by their large family, firmly ruled by Anna.

August continued for years to fell trees on the Grand Duke's estate. He is still a local celebrity. Last year, at a garden party to raise money to add an additional wing onto the local hospital, the present Grand Duke chose an old Scotch fir for him to fell into a limited space between two living trees. At first sight it seemed an easy job, offering no challenge. But as August walked round the trunk his memory was jolted by the sight of two healed scars of branches on different sides of the tree a few inches above the earth. A forgotten memory worried him. He thought hard. At last he remembered the two moles on the neck of the dark-haired woman at Sobibor. He studied the tree with added interest. Yes, it would be possible to divide them and leave things tidy, one protrusion on the severed trunk, the other on the uncut butt. Eagerly he set to work. The crowd applauded when the tree fell on the right place.

He was delighted he had retained his old skill. But that night he wondered what had happened to the eighteenth century executioner's axe from Lodz. Was it destroyed when the camps were bulldozed? If so, it was a wicked waste. He had never used a finer piece of steel and wished he had suggested they had given it to him instead of the money. He sighed, turned over and fell into a dreamless sleep.

Skating

Wilhelm Ruysch was born on January 23rd, 1900, in a large villa, built in 1880, on the outskirts of Amsterdam. His father was a Jewish merchant banker, his mother the daughter of the respected Doctor Fruin. At school he had average marks and remained in the middle of the class. His life was dominated by his friendship with an exact contemporary, Henri Mesdag, the dark-haired son of a successful lawyer. They often played silently together as children.

The staid young pair's life was governed by a ruling passion, only satisfied in winter, skating. Luckily a series of hard frosts at the beginning of the century enabled them to spend many free weekends and evenings on ponds and canals. At the age of ten they began to explore the multitudinous stretches of frozen water which dissected the countryside. They would return after dark, cheeks flushed, eyes sparkling. Every winter they discovered new journeys which they had planned, poring happily over maps, in the summer months. Holland's neutrality in the Great War allowed the country's youth to have an undisturbed education. Wilhelm, at the age of twenty-two, was a solidly built youth with a flat, red face, a straight back to his large head, and small eyes. He had worked adequately at school and the university and had pleased his parents, who never doubted their son would be the fifth generation of Ruysches to run the family merchant bank. His father started off his son's career by sending him to work for a business friend as a junior clerk. Wilhelm was still friendly with Henri, and they proudly boasted their knowledge of every canal within forty miles of Amsterdam. Both their parents saw no harm in their hobby, considering it infinitely preferable to running after girls. During periods of hard frost the young men would, on Sundays and during their holidays, wake at five, gulp down tea and skate all day and much of the following night. Their phlegmatic souls were stirred by the darkness, broken by distant lights sparkling with frost. They imagined themselves flying through an enchanted world of their own.

On January 6th, 1923, a national holiday, they set out at five o'clock to skate on a stretch of frozen water, neglected for many years. They planned to breakfast at a vaguely remembered lock-keeper's lodge. Nothing suggested their trip would be more or less memorable than their usual excursions.

They arrived before seven to find the lock gates closed, but bright lights shone through the frosted panes of the keeper's house. Encouraged, the young men took off their skates, climbed up the bank and knocked on the door intending to ask if they could buy bread, butter and hot milk. Oil lamps shining through the ice-covered windows reminded them of a Christmas card.

A plump, middle-aged woman wearing peasant costume opened the door. She looked such a typical country housewife neither of them noticed her features. She smiled, nodded and invited them to walk in. Taking off their caps they followed her, looking forward to their breakfast. They stood still, their mouths open with surprise; in front of them was the prettiest girl they had ever seen, sitting at the kitchen table with a mug in front of her. She had an oval face, one side reddened by the fire, the other white;

her teeth sparkled, her neck was long, her nose straight, her wrists elegant, her fingers delicate. She wore a long dress plucked in at the waist, but no bonnet. Her red hair was done up in a bun. She was equally astonished by the (to her) two good-looking young strangers and stood up, blushing. Embarrassed, she lifted her hand and in silence pointed to the two chairs nearest to the fire. The boys obeyed in a dream. Neither had ever seen such beauty. The girl's mother said, 'This is my Lise,' and began to heat the milk. Wilhelm and Henri at the same moment tried to win her attention. One said, 'The wind is cold on the canal', the other 'It is very cold on the canal.' They looked at each other in dismay. Each longed to show his superiority. Both felt their hearts beating rapidly. Lise burst out laughing; her white teeth made her prettier than ever. She asked where they came from, and when they said 'Amsterdam', said regretfully, 'Few skaters come here. It is out of the way. We live a quiet life.'

A long, awkward silence followed, broken when a triumphant Wilhelm blurted out, 'It was a hard frost last night. The ice is thick.'

The girl said sadly, 'My mother will not allow me to skate. She thinks I will break my legs.' The older woman nodded without speaking and put two mugs of boiling milk, plates of black bread and butter, a round cheese and a glass jar of strawberry jam on the table. The two young men rivalled each other in wondering whether the frost would hold. The girl sat silent, amused by their confusion. When they had drained their mugs they could think of no reason to stay.

The frost held, and the next Saturday Wilhelm said, 'Unfortunately I cannot go skating tomorrow. My exams are too near.' Henri nodded his head and said, 'I won't go alone.' They met at the lock, each carrying a bundle of flowers, frozen stiff by the icy air. Henri said, 'If I lied to you, you lied to me.' Wilhelm nodded his head. 'That is true. We are both to blame.'

Without smiling they gave their frozen offerings to the girl who tried to hide her laughter, while her mother welcomed them with a pot of her special raspberry jam. The elder woman was worried that her daughter seldom met anyone but farm-hands. These young men from Amsterdam looked rich. Three days later Henri collapsed with a serious attack of pneumonia. Wilhelm, ashamed of his pleasure at his best friend's illness, visited Lise every Sunday.

He sat one evening six months later, gazing hopefully at his bald, bent, bespectacled, short-nosed, neat little father who looked as if he had been born behind a desk. Plucking up his courage Wilhelm said in an unnatural voice, 'I would like to marry.'

Cold eyes looked at him, and a low voice asked, 'What is her name?'

'Lise.'

'Her surname?'

'I do not know if she has another name. Her mother is a lock-keeper's widow.'

'We will discuss the matter with your mother this evening.'

Wilhelm sighed. He had hoped to get round his father but his mother was a different matter. She held the family to be of supreme importance and knew not only the names of third cousins but every detail of their lives. When they met in the evening her hair seemed drawn back tighter than ever, her lips were thin and her eyes hard. She opened the conversation as the three of them sat on upright chairs at a round table.

'Why do you wish to disgrace your family?' She gave examples of other disastrous marriages between unequals.

Wilhelm stopped listening. He had no intention of marrying any other girl. After listening politely for ten minutes he asked if they had made a final decision. The pair looked at each other in silence and nodded their heads. Wilhelm asked: 'Can I visit her once a month?' His father replied without looking at his wife, 'Definitely not.' They stood up and walked out of the room.

To his mother's distress, this pliant young man, who had always done as he was told, ceased to eat and became pale and lifeless. His work in the bank deteriorated, his hair fell out. Two doctors, after long consultations, came reluctantly to the conclusion he was crossed in love. His puzzled father, who had never been in love or aware he had ever seen a lock-keeper's daughter, told his son to look at the matter sensibly and pull himself together. Wilhelm replied sadly, 'I have respected your wishes, I cannot help it if I have no appetite.'

The boy gradually lost weight until his worried mother found it difficult to sleep and began to grow thin herself. His father, pestered by a sick woman, fearful of his son's death, called a family conference, attended by two doctors. The eldest said in a low voice, 'You may not realise it, but cases of the young dying of love are not as rare as might be expected in our country; beneath placid exteriors we have deep feelings.' He believed Wilhelm was in a bad way. If they wished him to live he should be allowed to marry, despite the girl's low birth. He ended by saying, 'I am old enough to know that conventional marriages are not always happy.'

His remarks created an awkward silence. They were followed by a discussion which decided that Wilhelm should be sent to Belgium; his father had connections in Bruges. If in three months the boy was still in a decline they would reconsider his future.

He went to Bruges. His health failed to improve. Five

months later he married Lise. Only his family attended the wedding. His parents put a small announcement in the Amsterdam papers which implied their son had married a Belgian girl.

Lise did not love her husband but was grateful to him for taking her away from the lonely little house. She was intelligent and decided to learn how the smart women in the town dressed so that she could imitate their clothes. The beautiful unknown girl, staring with her nose pressed against the glass of fashionable shops astonished shop-keepers. Certain impressionable young men, fascinated by her looks, wondered where she lived and tried to follow her home. She always gave them the slip. Nobody ever found out who she was or where she lived.

She made her small house in a side street tidy and neat, designed and cut the curtains and covered the cushions. Every evening she stitched and sewed while Wilhelm sat opposite gazing in silence and loving admiration. She thought illness caused by his passion for her had taken something out of him. Since their marriage he seldom smiled. She often thought as they sat together, how lucky she was to live in a big town where she could happily amuse herself each day, but she could not help feeling disappointed at Wilhelm's listlessness and lack of enthusiasm. One evening she told him, smiling, gently clapping her hands, she had a secret. 'I am pregnant.' He nodded. 'You have been married seven months, it is to be expected. All the married girls I know soon become pregnant.'

'You don't seem very interested,' she said, in a faltering voice on the edge of tears.

'Well, it is usual, isn't it?'

'I suppose so,' she said, bending over her sewing.

She immediately started making little white dresses, changed her window-shopping and spent her time gazing into smart baby clothes shops. She had a good memory and was able to copy anything she thought pretty. It never occurred to her to ask her husband to buy her the expensive white cashmere shawl she gazed at every day with intense longing. Indeed it never occurred to him to buy her anything.

The child was due in February when ice for the second time played a part in Lise's life. Two days before her expected confinement she slipped on the icy snow and fell hard on the pavement. Her labour pains began. She was carried to a hospital where she gave birth to a little girl, later christened Jacqueline. The beautiful girl who had sat in the cottage dreaming of romance as she gazed at the empty canal, thought of nothing but her daughter. In the three following years she bore a son.

Wilhelm did not appear to notice. His father and mother decided their son was an idiot. To begin with he had insisted on marrying an unsuitable girl and when he had done so and she had given him four beautiful children he was not interested. What did he want?'

After five years the banished family was allowed to return to Holland. Lise's maternal qualities, neatness and efficiency had impressed her parents-in-law on their annual visits.

After their return to a large house next to Wilhelm's father, Lise became worried about Jacqueline, who could barely speak when her younger brothers were already reading. The child was taken to a distinguished doctor who wrote a report saying that while the child was backward she was not abnormally slow. 'I have tested her reactions and believe patience is necessary.'

Lise was not reassured and did everything she could to teach her little daughter by coloured cardboard letters and pictures of cats and dogs. The lovely eyes remained vacant. Lise would often weep with despair that her beautiful little girl was abnormal.

After a year the doctors admitted the girl was mentally retarded. Her mother continued to look after her and behave in every way as if she was normal. Luckily, her younger children all appeared, despite their mother's fears, to be ordinary. Their eyes sparkled and none of them showed any signs of mental disability and Lise was sure Jacqueline had been affected by her pre-natal slip on the ice. She was to blame for her daughter's condition.

Jacqueline was sent to a 'private school' where she sat all day playing with dolls. Every year she grew more beautiful, but Lise had to confess to herself she was happier when her daughter was out of the house. Whenever the mad girl looked at her Lise blamed her own clumsiness. What hurt her most was that she often heard friends murmuring, 'The mother and daughter look like twins.'

A startling change occurred in Jacqueline's character when she was twelve; her placidity was replaced by flirtatiousness. She would approach strange boys in the street and kiss them. Once she disappeared from school for a whole day. Her headmistress said if it happened again she could not continue to be responsible for her. It happened again. She was sent to the most famous general practitioner in Amsterdam, a man famed for morality, the father of nine children. He examined her. What happened was not known outside the family circle but it was whispered that the doctor wrote a stiff report, stating in shocked terms, 'Jacqueline has passions unnatural for her age which I regret she was unable to restrain even in my surgery. Fortunately a nurse was present. I suggest that she should be kept under strict supervision.'

Lise was made unhappier by her husband's lack of interest in his daughter and the other children and the attitude of his family who, despite their formal politeness, made sure she never forgot she was an outsider and was responsible for her daughter's madness. Sometimes they whispered together with averted eyes. Lise was certain they were talking about her and was irritated at their attitude that it was lucky madness had struck a girl and not one of the sons. The Second World War broke out when Jacqueline was sixteen. The next year the Germans invaded Holland. The Bank immediately suffered. The Nazi loathing of Jews ensured its future was bleak. Wilhelm's income was reduced, their servants left, one of them shouting, 'Bah, you filthy Jews!'

Lise began to cook; it was a relief.

At this time, a frightening moment for the Jewish community, Jacqueline caused a scandal by jumping on a postman. Another family conference was called. The dangers of anti-semitism were discussed. The family decided that they should live very quietly, give up all luxuries, dismiss all but the oldest servants. Lise's protests were listened to in silence when it was proposed that the only thing to be done was to put 'the mad girl into the State lunatic asylum at Apeldoorn as quickly as possible'.

Wilhelm never spoke even when his daughter's fate was discussed. Lise was furious but he invariably disappointed her whenever she needed him. She had known for years that the flushed, handsome boy who had appeared in her mother's kitchen, bringing her hope of a wider life, had become a dullard. The revolutionary spirit which had made him insist on marrying her had died. She decided he had always been conventional at heart. His loyalty to her had taken too much out of him and he was trying to make amends to his family in every way, even if they wished to commit his daughter to a public asylum. She loathed the family conferences: the self-satisfied relations sitting complacently round a shining mahogany table in their best clothes, the women pursing their lips but never speaking, smugness on their faces as they nodded at their husbands' remarks even if they were contradictory. The men, with one exception, had spoken as if they hated Jacqueline. Lise wanted to say that she did not see that making love mattered if it made her daughter happy but checked herself, knowing such words would make the relations even more unsympathetic.

When Lise made an involuntary movement of protest at the end of the meeting her father-in-law turned to her sternly and said, 'I am afraid there is no alternative. It is a pity she is not normal, but she is not, and would, if she is not shut up, draw attention to us at a time when we must behave with discretion. Her appearance alone excites discussion. You must see it is wise that she should enter a state institution. A private home suggests we have money to throw away. The Nazis will take note and oppress us.'

Lise had to clench her fists not to scream at them, 'All you think of is money.' She blamed herself afterwards for not having spoken, but she knew nothing she said would have changed the family's mind. She visited Jacqueline twice a week. To her surprise the girl appeared perfectly happy and laughed at her mother, her nurses, the mad patients and the old ladies who screeched delightedly. Lise, without servants, had to look after her sons before and after school, and do the cooking and housework. Her husband gave up his job and spent most of his time in the house. They seldom went out.

One evening in the beginning of 1943 Wilhelm came home after a visit to his parents with a twitching face, which only occurred when he was very worried. Lise took him by the hand and led him to his favourite armchair by the fire, where he smoked a pipe each night before going to bed. Worried, she knelt at his feet. 'What is it?' He looked at her and stammered, 'The Germans are going to take all the inhabitants out of the asylum and send them to the East.' Lise jumped up, put her hands over her mouth. 'When?' she said, and fainted.

The next day she had a high fever. The doctor came and gave her sedation. Her husband's aunt came and sat with her and did not leave her until she was replaced by her mother-in-law. She realised dimly that the family feared she might make trouble for them and had decided to imprison her. But whenever she asked about Jacqueline she was given a drink. A relation never left her.

During the time when Lise was living in her twilight world, a company of Germans with lorries filled with canvas-covered mattresses drew up outside the asylum. A captain was in charge. He led his men into a downstairs room in the forbidding looking building. It was filled with old women, some only in nightgowns, who shrieked and yelled. The German later reported: 'My men had no alternative but to pull certain patients forcibly out of the building. Fortunately the majority were obedient, but a small minority obstinately refused to obey orders. This forced our men to place the most violent on mattresses in the backs of lorries and cover them with other mattresses on which were laid other patients. The system worked and only two of the oldest women on the lower layer were dead when we reached the railway station. Loading the remainder into the trucks created further difficulties and further objectors had to be quietened in order to embark them.'

The Germans were more shocked than they admitted and realised it would be wise to treat the madmen differently if they were to get them on the train without causing an unpleasant local scandal. A hundred and twenty nurses were ordered into the recreation room and asked to volunteer to help take the patients east. Thirty put up their hands. It was not enough. A German police officer, F. A.

Aus der Funter, selected another thirty girls and ordered them to collect their belongings. The nurses were allowed to take a suitcase and four separate wagons at the end of the train were at their disposal. 'You will be more comfortable than your patients who you can visit at the stops. The wagons have been modernised to carry SS personnel and orderlies. Once you have delivered your cargo you will be returned here. You will each have two blankets.' The matron said she could not agree to the nurses having preferential treatment to the patients and that it was essential that two of them should go in each truck with their patients. The German captain shrugged his shoulders and indifferently agreed.

The matron also asked if the passive and younger patients could be put on the train first. Some of them were young men who, it was said, had pretended to be mad to avoid becoming soliders. Before getting into the lorries they stood whispering to each other; others walked up and down; another group sat waiting to do what they were told. Thirty-five of these 'passives' were packed into each wagon. A tight fit. The lorries returned for a second load; they were also 'comfortably fitted in'. The station master said that despite the cold weather, they would be crushed and over heated, and opened the ventilators. The military shut them.

The Germans left until the last the 'violent' wings filled with padded cell patients. The nurses said they would be difficult. This was no exaggeration. Patients of both sexes fought and tore their clothes off. The Captain's report read: 'We had no alternative to closing the wagon doors on the lunatics' fingers. A great deal of noise resulted. I ordered the doors to be reopened and the lunatics beaten back. A senior nurse insisted on entering the trucks; no fingers were inserted and the doors closed smoothly.'

Jacqueline had been a special case in the hospital; allowed to wander about at will. Injected with drugs which pacified her sexual instincts, she had been as harmless as a child and had sat happily with any companion, laughing all day long. At other times she had sat in the garden clapping her hands at fellow patients exercising themselves. Disasters amused her; when an old woman fell over, or if two young men fought, she would shriek with laughter. She had been no trouble and did everything she was told. The nurses all said what a pity that a girl with a body they would have given their souls to have, had no mind. The Germans found her eating quietly in a kitchen. A nurse put a blanket round her and put her, laughing, in a truck with eleven men and ten women – all violent cases – and two nurses. They set off with the ventilators shut.

The train crawled. The journey to the East took six days. The wagons were only opened to allow the nurses to get in and out. Men and women died and rotted on the journey. Once a day bread or biscuits and bottles of water were pushed through the ventilation holes. The nurses, who luckily all had medical bags, injected, calmed, distributed the food, fed the men in strait-jackets. At every stop they begged the Germans to pull out those who had died on the first day. The stink of the putrifying corpses was terrible; they refused, held their noses and tried to hurry the train driver on, to rid the station of an embarrassment.

Jacqueline enjoyed the journey and sat laughing at the screaming, strait-jacketed men. She ate all the bread she could get and after the first night slept happily, with her head on a dead woman's stomach. The smell reminded her of an old lady – a friend of her grandmother – who could not stop farting. She found the voyage amusing; she could not understand the suffering of her companions.

The stink was beyond belief. The nurses were frozen, white-faced, but Jacqueline felt well. Many comic things had amused her. Once a man stood up screaming at the top of his voice, violently pulled his clothes off and threw them at different people in the carriage. Two nurses tried to constrain him; it was no good. His arms and legs were made of iron. Eventually he sat down, pulled off his socks and slippers and stood up stark naked. Not once had he stopped shrieking. With a look of intense concentration he walked over bodies in a corner, clambered up to the small ventilation window covered with barbed wire and tried to get out. Time and again he pushed his head forward and each time he was forced back with a torn head and face. Once he fell onto his back, blood spurting from his nose, but leapt up and tried again.

Jacqueline cried with laughter; she had never seen anything as funny as when the two nurses tried to sit on him. He had jumped up and knocked them both down. She was also delighted when she noticed that the nurses dragged the newly dead men into a corner and tried to undress them. Jacqueline had always loved playing with dolls and in the carriage there was now a new doll every day whom she could treat exactly as she liked, her own playthings. She would turn them over, undo the backs of their dresses if they were women; their coats or strait-jackets if they were men, and throw the clothes to her companions.

The nurses allowed her to do what she wanted. Neither of them looked at her. They seldom slept and ceaselessly bandaged fingers and self-inflicted wounds. They wondered if the nightmare would ever end. They had no pills for Jacqueline and when she had undressed the two dead men she went on playing with them, especially at night when the nurses could not see what she was doing. One huge man died one morning and she spent a happy afternoon dressing and undressing him. He was very heavy but she was proud of her new strength and played with him incessantly until eleven o'clock when she fell sound asleep for twelve hours. The next morning, when she wished to start her game again, and was upset to find that the doll was completely stiff and his arms immovable, she could not understand what had happened and cried with rage. Luckily the nurses dragged a newly dead woman into the death corner and Jacqueline was able to undress her and, laughing, distribute her clothes.

Another thing she found funny was when the nurses blocked their noses with cotton wool. One afternoon the screams of two men in strait-jackets, jumping about like fish on a bank, amused her.

When at last they arrived, five men and four women lay dead. After the train stopped the doors were flung open and uniformed men with whips looked in and then backed away, holding their noses and shouting at the top of their voices. Eventually some of the quieter male lunatics in other trucks were brought up and whipped until they pulled the dead bodies out of the carriages. At last the train was empty and the lunatics were led out of the station to a number of waiting lorries. The nurses, protesting, were taken away. A senior officer, wearing a peaked cap, came up to Jacqueline who was standing against a pillar watching the sights and led her to a van waiting with its back doors open. She did not want to get in and, looking at him carefully, was struck by his funny peaked hat which he had forced down over his nose. He looked silly. She put her finger under the brim and jerked it off. He looked at her with amazement, as if he could not believe his eyes. At last he raised his short stick and struck her hard on the forehead. It hurt. But the sight of his bald head overcame the pain and she burst into fits of laughter. Three men with whips appeared and were ordered to put her into one of the vans. She fought them like a tiger, and every time they thought they had her, would, like Houdini, slip out of their hands and kick them in the stomach or in the throat. Two more guards joined in and she was overwhelmed. The man whose hat had been knocked off was standing shaking, white-faced. When she was at last secured he shouted that she should not be put into a van but dragged by a rope behind it.

A rope was wound around and around her arms and body until she was trussed up like a swaddled baby. She thought it funny to be tied up. In a moment she would exert her muscles and break the ropes. She had always been able to do this trick which had impressed her fellow companions. She started to laugh again and screamed loudly as the van moved off. It was fun being pulled along but ceased to be amusing when she hit a stone. They went faster and faster. She screamed with pain when it rounded a corner on two wheels and threw her against a wall by the road. The driver drove furiously at full speed and knocked down two Jews on the road to the prison camp. When it arrived Jacqueline was dead.

Back at the station the fifty-nine nurses (one had died on the journey) were shut in a waiting room where they had been given large tureens of bread and soup. Utterly exhausted, many did not bother to eat but fell asleep, their heads sprawled on the table. Others could not forget the terrible sights and walked up and down, aware life could never be the same again and they would for ever be haunted by the memories of dying defenceless lunatics.

Meanwhile the second-in-command, Major Sturm, was deciding what to do. He read the reports in front of him and telegrams wired from stations where officers claimed to have peered into the carriages to see that the prisoners had not escaped. Now he had to write a report on the nurses' conduct and recommend if they would be of use in the prison camp. He noticed that all the reports, without exception, dwelt on the 'wonderful', 'impressive', 'incredible', 'praiseworthy' conduct of the nurses. Apparently none of them had shirked the endless hours of nursing the lunatics or had shouted for food. On the other hand they had angrily begged for bandages, morphine etc. That was the only complaint.

He read that the train had pulled thirty trucks with seven hundred lunatics jammed inside. Over 35 per cent had died on the journey. A number of others had gangrene due to the dirt and cold. All the reports spoke of the bad condition of those in strait-jackets and one report went so far as to recommend that men should not be tied up in strait-jackets for such a long journey. The Major wrote beside this suggestion: 'I hope this officer will be reprimanded for an unrequested comment.' Another report by a lieutenant stated that the condition of the train on arrival was filthier than anything he had ever seen. He added he was a countryman and had frequently driven animals to the abbatoir. He had taken the responsibility of ordering all the carriages to be hosed out when they had been shunted into a siding. Unfortunately they still smelt; no amount of water seemed to lessen the appalling stench. He suggested that all the woodwork should be limed despite the ill effect on the timber. Otherwise he was frightened diseases could break out and spread beyond the prison; this would be serious.

The four German lieutenants who had been in charge of the Ukranians concluded their report with the unanimous hope that the lunatics should not in future be sent in trains for days on end. Surely such prisoners could be shot at the other end or thrown out of the train at some desolate period along the railway line. The arrival of a train load of screaming or dead lunatics had had an unfortunate effect on the Ukranians, who for the first time refused to do their duty. The four officers all agreed the conduct of the nurses was beyond praise and they hoped they would be rewarded for the calm way they had dealt with a difficult situation.

Major Sturm read all their reports and sent them off to his commanding officer. His conclusion was:

> It is undoubtedly true that the nurses behaved with exemplary efficiency; however, if these women are used as further servants of the Reich there is surely a danger they will discuss many of the unpleasant details which resulted from the exceptionally long time the train took to complete the journey. Exaggerated rumours could spread around Germany and cause harmful discussion. My recommendation is that I should order their elimination as soon as possible. Meanwhile they are confined in a rear platform waiting room in the station. The windows have been boarded up.

The next day Major Sturm's telephone rang. He was told his recommendation had been accepted. He was praised for not having, in the interests of the German nation, given way to sentimentality. He was ordered to shoot the nurses and have them buried that night.

The party

A number of questions were put to an aristocratic German army psychologist during his interrogation after the war. They concerned a sequence of events at Janowska concentration camp in 1942. He was asked about a report he had written after a visit to the camp dealing with an evening party given by SS officers. The guests were young and pretty Jewish prisoners. He did not condone or condemn the behaviour of the officers but advised the liquidation on arrival of female prisoners of beauty or attractive personality. His argument was simple; such women caused trouble and undermined discipline in the camps. He escaped before his sentence was announced and it was rumoured that he lived for fifteen years in Central America.

The most dreaded officer in this infamous camp was the large, fair-haired, red-faced, small-eyed Captain Bilhaus, a crack shot and a sadist. Two days after his arrival he concluded the evening inspection by shouting in a jovial voice that, in his opinion, the prisoners were a lazy, dull lot. He intended to wake them up the next day by a jest they might not enjoy.

It turned out that his idea of fun was to lie with a small bore repeating rifle on the floor of a flat-roofed building next to the public lavatory, overlooking the prisoners' exercise ground in the centre of the living quarter. The next morning, as a group of prisoners stood talking, stamping their feet, an old man, Isaac Badrum, suddenly clapped his hand to his bulbous nose. The bulb had disappeared. Nobody had heard a shot. A few seconds later another bullet missed its target and banged into the side of one of the huts. The third was successful, and took the tip of a finger of an elderly prisoner with a bad cold who was blowing his nose. Unfortunately he had extended the fingers of his right hand, which held a filthy piece of linen, in the manner of a refined lady holding a porcelain tea-mug. Before the prisoners knew what was happening two more shots were fired. The first one removed the lobe of a man's ear, the second the boot end of an eighteen-year-old boy. By a miracle the bullet missed his big toe. The impact knocked him over as cleanly as if he had been hit on the jaw by a professional boxer. That was enough, the prisoners disappeared into their huts with the speed of water running out of a basin.

The evening inspection was taken by the Captain. The prisoners shivered when he arrived with a sergeant, both in the best of humours and roaring with laughter. The nineteenth prisoner inspected was No. 11826; his red nose had been shortened by the first shot. The Captain stopped in front of him, roughly tugged the dirty bandage off his face and said in a voice thick with pleasure, 'What use are you without the end of your nose? Answer, please.' The old man's mouth opened; no words came out. Nobody moved.

After a moment Bilhaus slowly raised his hands: he was enjoying himself. His fingers closed gently round the neck of 11826. They gradually tightened. With a jerk he lifted the old man off the ground and shook him backwards and forwards until his face went blue and his wounded nose gushed blood. After a time Bilhaus threw the limp body like a sack of potatoes onto the tarmac. With a satisfied

114

smile on his face he continued the inspection. By the grace of God the young man shot in the boot had managed to repair it; he was passed without a word. Unfortunately, you cannot quickly replace or hide a finger end or an ear lobe. The two wounded men had their bandages pulled off before Bilhaus strangled them. At the end of the inspection he shouted in an exultant voice, 'We have no use for cripples here.'

He played his shooting game whenever he was bored. The prisoners learned not to stand in sections of the exercise yard visible from the flat roof. It did not help much; if the lieutenant was in a bad temper he would strangle a prisoner without bothering to give a reason.

Another famous joker was Major Dortenbach. He came into his own at the beginning of March on the first evening of the Purim celebrations. Pathetic efforts had been made to adorn the little prison children with ribbons or pieces of coloured handkerchief. The Major collected six Jews whom he said looked 'infectious', told them it was his duty to stop the spread of diseases and ordered them to lie all night on the ground; by morning they had been frozen to death. Pleased by his originality, he picked out the next night another eight sickly prisoners. They were ordered to spend the night in water barrels. In the morning they were dead blocks of ice. Their companions were ordered to cut them out.

The prisoners knew they might be killed for no reason at any moment: why they wished to live I do not know, but they clung to hope although daily preparing themselves for death.

On November 25th, 1944, Dortenbach and Bilhaus selected from the women's quarters twenty-four of the prettiest girls in the camp who, certain they were going to be shot or gassed, cried as they kissed their friends goodbye. They were all young, between seventeen and

115

twenty-one, and were, perhaps because of their looks, not as thin as the rest of the female prisoners. Camp life was promiscuous, morality is killed by hunger, sex with the Germans was not uncommon. If a German officer fancied a girl he would give her extra rations and try and seduce her, often with success.

To their surprise, the girls were not shot or taken to the gas chamber, but marched off to the officers' barracks where they were divided into four parties and led off by young officers to a momentarily empty wing of the officers' quarters. They were shown over small bedrooms and bathrooms and ordered to be ready for dinner in forty-five minutes. Their prison clothes had to be thrown into the passage outside their rooms. They would then have quick baths, wrap themselves in towels and wait in their bedrooms until nurses came round with an assortment of dresses. They could take their choice.

The bewildered girls, uncertain of their fate, did what they were told, except Sonia Monckenberg, a member of a rich Hamburg family. All her life she had been acclaimed as a beauty. 'Maybe,' her parents said, 'but she is not easy.' When she was fifteen they had complained about her passionate love of music and grumbled that directly she came home from school she would run up to the nursery, put on records and sit with a faraway look in her eyes. If her younger brothers complained, she would, without a word, carry the gramophone off to her bedroom. Her father, a rich and cultured timber merchant, would not have minded if she had any other interests. She had none, and had to be forced to comb her hair.

When she was seventeen, and nicknamed 'the Italian beauty', many would-be admirers – whom her mother called 'suitable' – thronged around her. Sonia ignored them. Her one ambition was to go to concerts or listen to the violin or piano in private houses. When she was

nineteen she announced one morning at breakfast that she
had fallen in love with a pianist called Bernard. She did
not know his surname. Her parents' disappointment
turned to dismay when they learned their black-haired,
black-eyed, straight-nosed, long-armed daughter, the most
beautiful girl in Hamburg, had chosen a half-bald hunchback of thirty-four, five foot four small. Sonia told them
she loved and had made love to him but was happy to go
on living with her parents until 'he is a success. Do not
worry, he will be, and we will have a flat of our own.' Her
mother cried. Her father told her to be sensible and
remember she was ruining her chances, 'nobody else will
now marry you.' She said, 'That's all right, I do not want
to marry anyone else.'

The war began. She worked in a children's home and
only saw her lover on Saturdays and Sundays. But her love
increased. He seemed to her to be the personification of
the beauty of music.

Her momentary return to civilisation in the officers'
wing made her think of Bernard. She was unable to resist
temptation before changing. She slipped between the white
sheets and remembered how she had loved him. It seemed
he was with her. She relaxed and fell asleep but did not at
once dream of her beloved; instead she was in her old
home, in her own bed, her father and mother upstairs, her
two brothers in the next room. She felt secure. Her dream
changed. She was at a dance – her lover had never been to
one – he appeared and told her she was the most beautiful
girl he had ever seen. She flung her arms round his neck,
only to wake up and find a young, red-haired German
pushing his tongue into her mouth. She pushed him off,
and would have screamed with horror if her mouth had
not been dry with disgust. To her surprise he did not hit
her, but put on his cap, saluted and said he would call for
her in twenty minutes. She would find, on the table at the

117

end of the bed, an evening dress, rouge, powder and silk stockings.

Sonia was determined to resist enjoying herself in any way but found to her horror she longed to wear silk stockings again. She resisted temptation by tearing them into bits. The powder was equally hard to resist. This was puzzling. She hardly used it at home. She hid the box behind a jug of water. She thought of undressing and going back to bed but that would be cowardly, and anyhow would not fit in with her plans. There was no alternative to wearing the pretty dress, and she was outraged at her pleasure and excitement. She was surprised and disgusted by her weakness and determined whatever happened not to relax and enjoy herself. She had not realised how weak she had become.

At seven-thirty an unrecognisable collection of elated girls, with washed hair, clean underclothes, new stockings, dresses and shoes were escorted downstairs into the officers' mess or heaven. The room had two fires, hot pipes, a long table covered with a white cloth on which stood eight silver candlesticks. Major Dortenbach stepped forward, bowed and kissed the hand of all the girls except Sonia, who kept her arm by her side. He took no offence but bowed politely. The waiters were eight batmen. Two good looking young nurses acted as hostesses. The officers' plan was to make their guests feel at ease and believe it was a normal dinner party. Most of the girls felt unreal, shocked; a few pulled themselves together and were looking forward to a good meal and saving their lives by winning the affection of a young, handsome German officer. Sonia and others were determined to die rather than submit. She whispered to those she decided were the most reliable girls, to keep clear heads and not drink wine or spirits. The majority did not know what to think; they had disappeared into an unreal dream. It was confusing to be at one momemt in grubby clothes in a filthy, bugridden ward, and the next in a beautiful, warm dining room wearing a dress and silk stockings and reassuringly feeling powder and lipstick on their faces.

To the girls' surprise, the officers ignored them and remained at the other end of the room. A tray loaded with apparently harmless fruit juice was handed round. The girls took the glasses, some with pleasure, others with disappointment. It did not enter their minds it had been laced with methedrine. Its effect was startling. The present pushed the future out of their minds and even the few who had been determined to enjoy themselves found they looked with interest across the room at the smart young transformed officers in dress uniform who stood quietly talking together.

After the fruit juice, champagne was served; none of the girls, even Sonia, refused it. Her hand disobeyed her mind and took the glass. By now the girls were piqued the officers paid no attention to them. This subtle welcome was due to the advice of a young army psychologist visiting the camp to study the effects of prolonged discomfort, separation of families, imprisonment, solitary confinement and knowledge of certain death. He was a smart, glib young man of thirty, whose presence was accepted by the officers because of his royal connections and the fact that his father had been a First World War General. He argued that if the girls were rushed, they would become antagonistic, frightened and the evening would turn into a disaster. He suggested that they should be given a bath, a pretty dress, and when they came downstairs, disguised methedrine to break down their antipathies. He also said firmly it would be wise to offer them champagne which should also be lavishly served after dinner. A gramophone should play carefully selected records; after that it was up to the officers.

Although such parties were against the rules, they often took place in the camps. Frequently they resulted in short-lived liaisons, and occasionally in love. It was not unknown for infatuated officers to try and fake false deaths and smuggle their mistresses out. They were shot if caught.

After the champagne, the gramophone played a 'March'. The batmen – paid double wages for the evening – led the girls and the two hostesses to their places. The German officers – the majority – were in their twenties, knew they were taking a risk, but as the girls were to be gassed the following morning, did not doubt they would get away with it.

The feast began with turtle soup, followed by trout and steaks. The girls felt gay and excited, except Sonia, fighting a losing battle against enjoyment. Despite her thinness, her sparkling black eyes and beautiful face made her the belle of the evening. What startled and pleased the girls was that the young officers, following the advice of the psychologist, had only been given one drink before dinner. The girls were therefore more self-confident and felt attracted by the naive shyness of those who, the day before, they had considered devils.

With the fish they drank Hoch. With the steaks Château Cantermerle 1929, with the stodgy pudding, Château Climens 1928. The barriers fell, laughter filled the room, most of the girls felt blissful. One of them shut her eyes to enable her to open them again and prove she was not dreaming. She told a friend, who imitated her. The Germans roared with laughter and considered themselves benefactors. Only Sonia, with difficulty – for despite her good intentions she found herself studying the red-haired boy – retained her determination to resist temptation.

The gramophone played the psychologist's selections. The lights were turned off, candles lit. The waiters cleared away the food and withdrew. Sonia refused to dance but she could see the others clinging to their partners. She realised she had lost, but did not blame the other girls, she had nearly fallen herself and knew she must remain strong to maintain her honour. She felt wary of her feeling of elation. The red-haired boy of twenty-three told her about his younger sister; he had tears in his eyes as he said how much he loved and missed her. Sonia wondered if he could be the same young man who daily strutted around the camp slapping his leg with a stick and ordering old women and girls to be flogged or killed.

The waiters brought in more champagne. Bilhaus was the first to leave the room, pulling behind him a girl considered by the others to be 'simple'. Other couples began to slip away. Sonia's admirer, by now tearful and maudlin, said to her in a sad voice, 'You know, I had planned to sleep with you tonight, but you remind me of my sister and I cannot do it. I don't know why, but I feel sorry for you all, and will do what I can to help.' He led her to the bedroom, kissed her hands, looked down at them and went out locking the door. To her amazement she found herself wishing he had stayed. She slapped her cheek hard three times. What was wrong with her? Why was she excited?

During the night Sonia heard the clink of glasses, giggles, laughter as doors opened and closed. To begin with she felt angry, even furious, at her companions' lack of determination. Then she wondered if she was being honest and was, if she was truthful with herself, envious of their gaiety.

She slept in snatches and if she dreamed of home or her lover, woke herself up. By the early hours the methedrine had worn off. Her tolerance vanished. She started to organise her revenge. Her life did not matter, she did not mind how much she suffered; torture would deservedly punish her for her incomprehensible weakness at dinner. She lit a candle – the electricity had been cut off – but could find nothing in her room which she could use as a weapon. There must be something somewhere. But what? The china mugs were no use, there was nothing detachable. She thought of the window panes. Would it be possible to knock one out so it would not be noticed in the morning? Sonia decided to wait until the last possible moment so that her room would not become noticeably freezing. She lay thinking of her early life and her lover; as usual her heart ached. But for the Nazis, they would have been married. She knew she could never love a man again. Three months before she was taken away Bernard had vanished. Her heart stopped when she heard. Afterward she had woken up every night and wept till dawn. When she was arrested and thrown in a truck, her companions shrieked and groaned, she sat down in a corner, her back against the jolting side, unconscious of cold, discomfort, hunger, determined to maintain her dignity, die if necessary but never to submit.

Every day she had written a diary, not about her life in the camp but about her thoughts and her lover and the life she would have lived with him. She would have had two children, a boy and a girl. She kept it on top of her bed in the camp; and wrote on alternate pages in an edition of Nietze, allowed in the camp. She planned her last unwritten entry: 'I am willing to die. I tried to make the girls promise to resist, they failed out of weakness. I was also nearly weak. I am as bad as they are.'

She had conceived her momentary freedom as an opportunity to kill a Nazi, not caring that revenge was uncivilised. She loathed Hitler and all his followers. She dug her nails into the palms of her hands to stop herself screaming 'I hate you all, I hate you!'

At dawn she took her pillow and punched it through a

small window pane. As she had hoped, some long splinters of glass remained in the wooden frame. She carefully extracted one, and, with her tooth brush, broke off the other jagged remains until the paneless window was hardly noticeable. She pulled the curtain sideways. The room was cold anyhow; there was no wind to make it colder.

Half an hour later a loud voice shouted down the passage that the girls should 'get ready'. She hacked off a small piece of sheet, wrapped it around the glass and, placing the weapon between her breasts, changed into her formerly dirty prison uniform which had, ironically, been returned cleaned, ironed, neatly folded on a bedroom chair.

At six o'clock the voice shouted again in the passage: 'The truck is coming in fifteen minutes.' Punctually the guard arrived. One by one the doors opened and the girls were pushed out into the passage; sometimes force was needed. Nearly all of them had tears running down white faces smudged with make-up and lipstick. Sonia did not speak but walked on ahead. At the bottom of the stairs she noticed an argument going on under the light, outside the entrance. Her red-haired admirer and Major Dortenbach were surrounded by a group of officers; Captain Bilhaus was shouting, 'Don't let's be weak, they should be gassed.' He laughed and continued, 'I found it exciting having a girl who you know is going to be killed the next morning.'

'Be quiet!' shouted the Major as he looked furiously at the Captain. 'I disagree with you, and remember I give the orders here. Without question it is more amusing to keep them alive if they performed as well as they did last night. The time to gas them,' he added in a low voice, 'is when they cease to amuse.'

He walked in front of the snivelling girls and said, 'Ladies, it was our intention to dispose of you, but you pleased us so much by your behaviour last night that I have decided you should continue to live. Say nothing of what happened or I will know and you will die, understand? If you are good we will have another dinner. Back to your quarters.' He slapped his right boot.

'Thank you,' said Sonia, in a clear voice. 'May I thank you personally?'

The Major looked nonplussed. 'What do you mean?'

She walked towards him. He continued to look surprised. There had been an unusual authority in her voice. Stopping in front of him she smiled and said, 'May I kiss you on behalf of the girls?' A self-satisfied look came over Dortenbach's face. He smiled in a condescending way and leaned forward. She drove her piece of glass into his throat.

When the confusion had died down and the Major carried away, a captain ordered the soldiers to take the girls away and shoot them. The murderess was taken indoors for interrogation. The psychologist with good connections insisted on sitting in. She refused to give any answers except that she had acted to preserve the honour of humanity and to mitigate the shame of her companions who had given their bodies to monsters. No, she was not sorry her companions had been shot; they would have been killed anyway. The psychologist asked her a few questions. She answered truthfully, and without warning burst into tears, crying out, 'You killed my lover. I long to die. I do not mind if you torture me.'

The judgement of the four interrogators was that Sonia should be given to the sergeants to rape to death. The psychologist calmly disagreed; the scandal must be minimised or they would all suffer. She should be shot on the other girls' open grave. She was.

The psychologist considered the case interesting and made a full note of the affair.

Pig

I

Her first memories were shouts of 'Pig, Pig, Pig!' The word echoed through her childhood whenever her mother and two elder sisters wanted anything. If an upstairs book was needed, she was sent. If there was no room in the car on a visit to a local beauty spot, Pig was left behind. She always wore her elder sisters' clothes, and was often given their old toys. After she had passed her driving test, if a hamper had to be fetched from the station, she fetched it; if an important registered letter had to be posted, Pig posted it; if a dog had to be taken to the vet, Pig, smiling amiably, took it. A witty cousin said, 'Poor Pig is always sent on with the luggage.'

She was not piteous, enjoyed life and spent a good deal of time talking to servants, first in Sheffield, later in London and later still in her father's country house on the outskirts of Esher. After all, anything was better than reading. She always fell in with any plan for excursions or picnics (although she was always expected to pack up the picnic basket). In short, she was one of those happy natures who find life 'fun' and never take offence if they are asked out to dinner at six o'clock.

She won her nickname when she was born with a thicket of coarse blond hair. Directly she saw the new baby, her older sister, Cosima, said in a scornful voice, 'Oh, Mummy, she looks like a little pig!' The name stuck. Pig did not mind, she was easily amused. If anybody started giggling she could not help joining in, although she often had no idea what she was laughing at. If an old woman tripped over a stool she had to rush out of the room and stuff a handkerchief in her mouth to avoid exploding with mirth. She tried not to offend anybody if she could help it, but when her uncle fell over skating and broke his ankle, she collapsed. Nothing put her out; she accepted with good natured placidity the slavery of her adolescent years when her family, with the one exception of her father, Alistair, bossed her around. If he wanted anything he asked the nearest girl and firmly called his youngest daughter Pamela, never Pig. But the servants called her Miss Pig to her face and 'that pig' behind her back. Her father's success worried her; she could not help noticing that her mother and sisters changed, put on airs, annually made new friends and dropped old ones. Her life would have confused a less complicated, good-natured girl.

Her grandfather, the first Alistair MacIntosh, had been, she was told as a child, kidnapped and shipped to the Argentine. Whether this was true, she never knew. Her father was vague and embarrassed about the legend, while her mother dismissed it as nonsense. But undoubtedly Alistair had gone to South America, when he was only fifteen, to work as a navvy on the railway network then beginning to cover the virgin lands. He was a hard-working, serious boy, who only got drunk on New Year's Eve and soon won the overseer's respect and was promoted. He had the ability to understand figures and, at a very early age, earned a good salary which he saved and annually invested.

When he was thirty-five he married a fellow ex-patriot Scottish girl. They built a small ranch house which his wife turned into a vignette of the suburbs of Glasgow with lace curtains, a picture of Queen Victoria and an aspidistra in the window. His heart remained in his homeland where he sent his only son, Alistair, aged eighteen, to finish his education at 'The University'. It was a shock to the boy, used to the endless pampas, to be confined in 1886 to the foggy valley beneath the stark Edinburgh castle. He was homesick all his life for the empty lands he had known in his youth, when he could ride thirty miles in any direction without crossing a road.

The elder Alistair kept in touch with his schoolboy friends, some of whom had been as successful in England and Scotland as he had been in South America. They kept an eye on the boy; when he won a good degree they saw that he was well placed in one of their Sheffield steelworks. The second Alistair, like his father, started at the bottom and could say, and often did, that he had worked in every department of John Osbourne & Co. He had his family's virtues: in 1914 he became the chairman of a large company. At this period of the war, many complaints came back from the front of dud shells, bombs and ammunition, none of which were ever traced back to his firm. A down to earth man, with a clear mind, he was chosen to be a member of a committee Lloyd George set up to increase the efficiency of the manufacturers of armaments. From then on he was marked down by Whitehall as an ideal committee man.

His new position ensured that, for the first time in his life, he frequently visited London. His wife and family remained in Sheffield. He was forty-eight. Sixteen years before he had married Jessie, the pretty, musical, ambitious daughter of a Sheffield clergyman. They had four children. She picked her husband out as a man who would succeed, and take her away from the uncivilised, smoky town where, she was sure, her good taste and sensibilities were wasted. Jessie had a long wait. A son, Alistair, was born in 1900. Cosima, called after Wagner's wife, in 1903, Cecily in 1906 and Pamela in 1912. The MacIntosh home, originally in the country three miles from Sheffield, was a large Victorian stone house, enclosed in one and a half acres of ground. The Beardsley drawings in her bedroom shocked their friends. Gradually the countryside disappeared until the house was surrounded by buildings, but the garden with its tennis court was big enough to reserve the owners' privacy.

The second Alistair was a large, impressive man, with a square face, a blunt nose and a slit of a mouth, contradicted by large brown eyes which appeared to be good naturedly looking into the future. He was sound and practical, expressed himself slowly and learned to be the last speaker at committee meetings. After the war he went back to live in Sheffield. His elder daughters, nine and six years older than Pig, grew up in the town with girlfriends whose fathers were members of the local cabal. They seldom went to London where their father stayed in the Pall Mall Club. Jessie constantly pestered him to buy a town house, saying it was unfair to constrict the lives of his eldest daughters. The girls were not unhappy. They went to numerous local dances and parties and their tennis court ensured jolly afternoons when the sun peered through the smoke. Neither of the two eldest girls were pretty but were kindly described as 'good-looking'; each of them married when they were twenty. Cosima in 1923 and Cecily in 1926. In the same year their father was knighted for 'services to industry'. Their husbands never thought of leaving Sheffield, where they intended to succeed in 'steel'.

In 1929 the even tenor of their provincial life was broken. At the age of sixty, Alistair MacIntosh was, to his surprise, given a peerage in the New Year's Honours List and informed he would, after the General Election, be made a junior minister. Unfortunately, the Conservative

Party was defeated and Ramsay Macdonald became the Labour Prime Minister. His administration, undermined by the slump, only lasted two years; he then became a Conservative puppet. In 1931 Lord MacIntosh was asked to chair a committee to recommend and implement methods by which business confidence could be regained. After twenty-nine years Jessie believed she had reached her Eldorado. The family bought a house in Park Street, London, and another converted Tudor farmhouse near Esher. Pig's elder brother was given, and lived in, the Sheffield house. To her surprise and her sisters' annoyance Pig was told in 1931 she would be presented at Court by Lady Hammond-Graeme, who made her living out of the daughters of the nouveaux riches. This lady had a commanding presence, a hooked nose, minute eyes and an attentive little husband about half her size, often described as her little dog.

She never allowed him to be more than a foot away from her. The great day of the year was Queen Charlotte's Ball where she organised and paraded ambitious debutantes.

Her charges were prepared like cattle for an agricultural show. Plain debutantes from Lancashire and the Midlands had eyebrows plucked, hair re-arranged in the latest fashion, and flattering photographs taken by Cecil Beaton. Photographs of them appeared in the three smart social weeklies, The Tatler, The Bystander, and the Sketch, with whom Lady Hammond-Graeme had many complicated financial arrangements.

The duenna was expensive but, as she pointed out, 'if a girl is to marry well she must be seen'. She gave dinners paid for by parents, saw that young men danced with her charges at balls, told her pupils to be careful, dutiful, polite and firmly not to drink too much or dance too often with the same young man. It must be admitted the last temptation was seldom a problem for Pig. Occasionally she was asked, due to their father's importance, and much to Lady Hammond-Graeme's annoyance, to select, aristocratic balls.

Lady Hammond-Graeme often told Pig she laughed and spoke too loudly to be a social success and insisted that when she was amused, she should not throw back her head, open her mouth and roar with laughter, but smile elegantly. Her stiff young escorts soon decided that with her red face and coarse flaxen hair, it was unlikely she would marry well. Her dowry was known to be only twenty thousand pounds. She did have a few young, amusing, badly behaved, well born friends, who were amused by her infectious enthusiasm and pleased with the MacIntosh house in which her mother gave dinner and luncheon parties and the type of musical evenings which had seemed smart in Sheffield. Sadly they were considered side-splittingly funny in Mayfair. Pig's friends' ambition was to make a nervous, forty-year-old, thin violinist from Hungary with long, black hair laugh or cry by making faces at him. One day they succeeded; he put down his violin and stood, both hands hiding his eyes, in tears. He was dismissed. Her friends said, 'It's the end of the chase, we have killed our fox.' Pig found herself worrying if he had a wife and children.

She accepted without bitterness that it was her fate to receive stopgap invitations for dinner and replace at the last moment sick guests at weekends in grand houses. She was also a good tease for conventional mothers who were horrified at her loudness.

When Pig was nineteen she had an unhappy experience with a good-looking young man who had a bet he would seduce her. To her delighted surprise he danced with her all one evening, sent cut flowers the next day. He asked her to lunch, gazed into her eyes, told her he loved her. His friends conspired to make her drunk. A weekend later he crept into her bedroom and won his bet. She felt guilty the next day, miserable the following week as she sat waiting in vain for a telephone call. A good friend told her about the bet, she went to Sheffield, cried for five days and decided it was not the end of the world: her good spirits won and she returned to London. The incident made her cautious of her dancing partners and all young men. But afterwards she thought her experience had been worth it, her lover had looked so beautiful. She was not unhappy but regretted she had not fulfilled her mother's hopes. Later on it was rumoured that 'she was good natured'.

When she was twenty-three her father decided, with what the press called his 'solid North Country sense', that she was deteriorating, 'had lost her good name' and was likely to remain unmarried. He was not as worried as his wife as he knew his daughter had determination and character. He decided to help and arranged she should do social work in the East End four days a week. She was an immediate success and when she found motherless children cowering in a corner with bruises while a drunken father snored upstairs, she would shake him awake, force him to dress and come downstairs, to find his unrecognisable family in clean clothes, eating bread and jam on a recently scrubbed table. Wretched men, suffering from hangovers, shrank before a girl who told them exactly what she thought of them, which was nothing at all, and made it plain that unless they pulled themselves together she would call the RSPCC. Usually this threat worked for a week or two, but if a man had lost his job and wife and was on the dole, there was not much joy about, except on Friday evenings in the local.

In 1934 Lord MacIntosh became a Minister and his two sons-in-law moved to London, with jobs in the City. The family reunion meant Pig was often asked to take her nephews and nieces to the zoo, or Gunters, and to spend weekends in their London houses if they went away. She accepted and persuaded herself that she loved the serious, white-faced children, but she hoped her children would not all wear spectacles, and would take themselves less seriously than their cousins. But then, as she used to say, 'It takes all sorts to make a world.'

As she grew older Pig was increasingly called on to stand in as the hostess for her father's dinner parties. Her mother had come to London too late. Thirty years of provincial life had changed a lively, artistic girl into an uninteresting, shy provincial whom her husband's new associates found 'difficult'. Her daughter found it easier than she did to talk to elderly, less critical politicians who were often relieved to sit next to an easily amused, fair-haired girl with a fresh, red face. Without doubt as she grew older she became better looking.

When Pig was twenty-five she began to fear she would never marry. This was sad. All her life she had dreamed of having children and one night, after a ball where nobody, including a man she had thought was interested in her, had danced with her, she finally realised she would never belong to the London world and should never have left Yorkshire, where by now, she would have had a husband and children. How much better that would have been than occasionally looking after her wretched little nephews and nieces and working in the depressing East End. She cried herself to sleep but woke up in a better mood and decided, looking herself squarely in the mirror, that uglier girls than her had married. Certainly her life was depressing.

But what was the alternative? She liked music, her favourite composer was Wagner. His thunderous compositions filled her with confused excitement. But she had no musical ability. She had not the confidence or imagination to write and be a newspaper reporter, although Lord Beaverbrook had offered her a job one day at lunch. It is possible she would have devoted her life to good works and her forlorn mother if she had not picked up a telephone one day and heard her sister, Cosima, saying: 'Well, I will make Pig do it.' A voice at the other end said, 'Oh, but won't it be a bore for her?' To which her sister replied, 'No, I am sure she has nothing else to do. Anyhow, I think she is lucky to be asked to do anything.'

Pig felt blood rushing to her face and pushed her fingers against her forehead to try to expel the words from her mind. She failed, and decided to go away and start a new life. At least she would see something of the world, which would be better than living at the beck and call of sisters who despised her. Pig had realised by Cosima's voice that her sister only considered her an oddbody, fit to take children out to tea. Where was she to go? What was she to do? Her trust in her father saved her. She went to see him that night in the library. As she talked, she saw regret in his large eyes and realised, despite all his new, grand acquaintances, he had not changed much either, at any rate, not enough to stop him from understanding her suffering. He did not speak until she had finished but sat back in his chair looking glum. At last he said, 'I'm sorry, lass, all our lives are a bit of a mess now, you know, I should never have left Yorkshire. We can't be what we're not. I am a misfit at dinners as well. I don't laugh at the same things as the others. But you can't go back on what you have done. I will see what I can do.'

That night after dinner he drank two glasses of port before asking the elegant, military, Conservative Chief Whip where he could send an unmarried daughter of twenty-five. David Margesson looked him straight in the eyes, paused and asked, 'Do you want her married off?'

'Yes.'

'Well, at this time of year, try one of our European embassies. They usually have a few well connected unofficial attaches hanging about. If that fails send her to Vice Regal Lodge in the hills. I will arrange it. Any girl who's not a cripple is snapped up like a mayfly in India.'

Three weeks later Pig was told she was going to stay for one month in Berlin with the British Ambassador, Sir William Sanderson, who was enraged at the way England was being persuaded to distrust Hitler. He was glad to have an influential politician's daughter to stay and learn the true state of affairs. She was to visit youth clubs in Berlin and would bring a German girl back to England to her father's house for three weeks. Pig wondered what she would do with her, but it was no use worrying about things until you had to. The great thing was she was going away and might make new friends.

She felt nervous on the way to Berlin as she knew the Ambassador, greatly admired by the Prime Minister, was very solemn and serious. She hoped not to see too much of him. Her train arrived in Berlin at five o'clock; she was overwhelmed by the Rolls Royce and the second secretary who had come to meet her. He was a formal young man and asked her about the weather and what theatres she had been to in London. At the embassy she was immediately shown to a large bedroom; on the writing table lay a printed note saying the ambassador requested her presence at seven-thirty in his library. The meeting would be brief, guests arrived at eight-fifteen. Pig trembled, wondering how on earth she would find the library, and at seven-thirty started pacing nervously round the room trying to screw up courage to walk downstairs and find one of the terrifying servants to show her where it was. She had made up her mind and was about to open the door when there was a tap on the other side. Flinging it open she saw the young man who had met her at the station and felt a rush of friendship and relief; he bowed like a butler and led her downstairs in silence to a large room in which the ambassador sat writing. He did not look up until she was a yard from his desk. Then with rapid movements he put down his pen, took off his spectacles and walked round his desk to shake hands. Pig's heart sank a little at his weak handshake, sallow skin and drooping moustache. He led her over to the sofa and for the next quarter of an hour explained that the Nazi movement was misunderstood in England, Hitler only wished to return German minorities to their fatherland. She was not quite sure she understood what German minorities were or where they lived, but she nodded her head wisely, and continued nodding when Sir William went on, 'Unfortunately, reasonable German ambitions are distorted by warmongers.' Thinking he would go on talking, she relaxed and jumped with surprise when he suddenly said, 'You can play a part, for I am arranging for you to meet members of the princely German families, and will be giving a small dance for you tomorrow. All the young men you will meet are serving in the Army, so you will be able to judge, without any influence from me, as to the type of movement Nazism is.'

Pig could not help feeling rather important and smiled at the thought of how her sisters would envy her. She could not wait to write and casually mention the ambassador had given a dance for her. Sir William said sharply, 'What are you laughing at? How have I amused you?'

Pig jumped again, aghast he should think she was mocking him. Conciliatory words tumbled out of her mouth.

'No, yes. I mean, it's very kind of you. I am looking forward to it. It's very thoughtful of you.'

The next day she visited a youth club, unlike any she had been to in England. The girls, in green uniforms, lined up for inspection. She could not say she liked the military atmosphere.

In the evening she followed Lady Hammond-Graeme's advice and wore a long white dress with sleeves down to the wrists. This was wise as Pig's strong round arms were covered with the unfortunate hair that had won her nickname. She was not discouraged when she looked in the mirror, deciding that she could have looked worse; her lips and cheeks were naturally red. As usual she was nervous as she walked downstairs, and did not know what to do with her hands as she walked into the drawing room, five minutes before the guests were due to arrive. The ambassador's sister, Miss Sanderson shook her hand. She was a frightening hostess with a formal, stiff manner and was very shy, except in private, when she incessantly complained about the cold and the central heating which did not work, except in hot weather.

'We had better see, Miss MacIntosh, where you are sitting and then I will get Archie . . .' she pointed rudely Pig thought, to another young man, 'to tell you about your neighbours.'

She led Pig to a table on the right of the door, on which lay six plans of round tables, each seating ten people. 'I do not know how the dance will go. The rest of the secretaries and attachés will come in after dinner and tonight Sir William has said they can each bring a young lady so it should be a pleasant gathering. I understand he has also asked them to bring a few more friends we have met and approved, you have got to be careful about that – upper class Germans are more touchy than we are about who they meet, you know.'

Pig did not know; she had often thrown her clothes on and gone straight round to many last minute invitations.

'Well, here you are,' said Miss Sanderson, pointing to her name. 'Although the dance is in your honour, William thought it would be entertaining, although not correct, for you to sit between two young men. We have placed you between Prince Henry of Rothenburg . . .' She paused and added in an embarrassed voice, '. . . Archie will tell you about him, and Prince Augustus of Baden. I am sure they are both very nice but there are so many Baden princes I am not certain whether or not I have met this one. Archie, brief her please.'

Archie led Pig to a sofa and said, 'Shall we sit down?' He produced two pieces of crisp, folded embassy paper. On one was written 'HRH Prince Henry of Rothenburg' and on the other 'HRH Prince Augustus of Baden'. Beneath each name was written when they were born, educated, joined the Army, the names of their castles, fathers, mothers, brothers, sisters, all of which confused Pig whose father had told her, 'Remember, Germany is a republic and all titles have been abolished.' When she said this to Archie he smiled. 'You would not think so if you lived here.' He gave her a little red book and said, 'Here is the 1937 Almanach de Gotha which I will leave here, hide it behind that photograph of the King; refer to it later when you have to address letters correctly, and you are sure to get a lot of invitations.'

Pig looked in bewilderment at the first three sections of the small red book listing hundreds of princes, princesses, dukes, duchesses, counts and countesses in tiny print. 'Oh dear,' she said, 'would you mind if I asked you how to address my letters?'

'Not a bit,' he said with a smile which she was glad to see showed he was human.

The guests soon arrived, not one was late. She found herself being introduced to a lot of stiff, upright young men, all wearing brilliant uniform. They clicked their heels and kissed her hand. With difficulty she stopped herself giggling. When they sat down the Prince of Rothenburg bowed and turned to his left while the Prince of Baden, a tall, thin young man with dark hair, no chin and a large, round Adam's apple, turned towards her and asked her if she hunted; when she said no, he frowned and asked her where she lived. She said, 'London, and before that, Sheffield.' 'Sheffield?' he said in a surprised voice. 'Is not that an industrial town? I hunt in Leicestershire every year. I prefer the Quorn to the Pychley. It is a tragedy that the cavalry has ceased to exist as a weapon. You cannot boost your men's morale from a tank, like you can from a horse.'

Pig longed to laugh at the idea of soldiers' morale suffering at not seeing this leader, but checked herself, remembered Lady Hammond-Graeme's advice, smiled and looked impressed. Halfway through the roast beef Sir William appeared to give a secret sign; the young men, as one, turned and immediately started talking to their so-far ignored neighbours even if they were in the middle of a sentence. Pig thought they behaved as if they were obeying an order. She turned without expectations towards Prince Henry. He was tall and thin with wispy hair receding from his forehead, a long nose, and a jaw which sloped away at an angle as if deferring politely to his Adam's apple. She wondered if Adam's apples were a sign of aristocracy in Germany. He had sandy, colourless skin but his eyes made up for his defects. They were large, kind, brown like her father's, protruding a little, but reassuring.

He asked about London and whether she knew anything about Germany. She said no, she had only been to Berlin and would love to see the countryside. He looked at her sympathetically and said he liked the country best; their chief palace was in Rothenburg but he loved their smaller country house in the forest ten miles away, which was his home. His family had many houses. He had two younger brothers, both had children.

That night in bed she remembered how they had looked at each other. Surely her heart had never beaten so fast before. She had fancied a lot of good-looking young men but had never trusted or loved any of them or felt like she did now. Prince Henry had talked to her as if they were old friends. Everything had seemed interesting and she had, for some reason she did not understand, told him about her mother's sadness, and how her father had only been made a peer and minister a few years before, and that their change of life had ruined a previously happy marriage. Then, to her amazement, she heard herself telling him about her sisters and their children. There was nothing she would not have told him. She felt at ease, excited and happy. At the end of the meal Miss Sanderson led the ladies into the ballroom where a band was playing. Champagne and ices were laid out on a side table. Prince Henry soon came in with the other men and never left her, except when she had to dance the first waltz with Sir William, who trod on her toes; afterwards dancing with Henry was a dream. She fell in love, and when he asked to see her the next day, she shut her eyes – it all seemed too good to be true. From then onwards they talked together whenever they met, which was nearly every evening. Her friendship appeared to worry Sir William, who asked her to come to his library and told her Prince Henry could not marry her, she was unmediatised. She did not know what he meant but nodded, determined to enjoy every moment of her visit. After all, it was the nicest holiday she had ever had and all good things came to an end. One morning she realised she was returning to London the next day with the most beautiful girl in Germany, Princess Isabella Salm-Salm-Salm, who, she knew, would be laughed at because of her name. She had suggested that to use three identical family names would cause amusement. An attaché said respectfully, 'She comes from one of the noblest and richest families in Germany.' Pig still knew it would be a joke in London. But on the other hand the girl was so beautiful she might get away with it.

On the last morning she consoled herself with the knowledge Henry was coming to a farewell lunch. To Pig's surprise at nine-thirty she was sent for by the Ambassador who told her, pursing his lips doubtfully, that her goodbye meeting with representatives of the Berlin Girl Guides was cancelled. Prince Henry was calling to take her to see his mother and father. 'I take it,' Sir William concluded with a doubtful look, 'that you understand the implications of this gesture. But you may not have an easy meeting. I have cancelled Princess Isabella Salm-Salm-Salm's visit to England. She understands and asks me to congratulate you.'

Despite all the trouble she had caused, Pig noticed the Ambassador talked to her deferentially, and for the first time walked with her to his door and bowed as he opened it. She was flabbergasted, and stood, unbelieving, motionless. Could Henry really be going to marry a common little girl from Sheffield? She blurted out the question. Sir William frowned, shuffled his feet, and said, 'I do not think you should demean your father, but I should make it plain to you that if an offer of marriage is made you will only have the status of a morganatic wife.'

'Goodness, please do not go into all that, but I will be legally married, won't I?' Sir William looked embarrassed. 'Legally married, yes, certainly, that is, if you become a Catholic.'

'Why not, it is worth it, isn't it?'

Sir William frowned and continued, 'But your children will be morganatic and unable to succeed to the Princedom. Also I think I should explain your future husband, although he is the eldest son, will not be the next Prince of

Rothenburg, who will be his younger brother. Prince Henry was ill as a boy and has retiring manners.'

'Oh,' said Pig in surprise, and heard herself adding, 'I don't mind a bit. I want to marry him because I love him, not because he is a prince.'

Sir William looked carefully around before whispering, 'You know, you will not be in bad company. In England we do not go in for that sort of thing. In fact, if we had, King George VI could not have succeeded to the throne as Queen Mary belongs to a morganatic family.'

This tickled Pig's imagination and she snorted again, 'So, I'm in the same boat as Queen Mary, am I? That's good,' and she threw back her head, forgetting Lady Hammond-Graeme's orders, and roared with laughter. Sir William seized her hand, quickly shook it, gasped, 'Do not repeat what I have said, but in Germany I prefer Herr Hitler and his friends to the old school,' and darted back into his room.

Henry called punctually at eleven to take her to see his parents in a large, dark house with huge windows and high ceilings. The walls were covered with pictures of men in uniform, wearing swords. Colossal pieces of furniture adorned with brass filled the room. Pig was welcomed with polite pleasure. Henry's mother took her to a window, put both arms around her and kissed her. Pig was embarrassed. She thought the woman was acting when she told Pig in a voice she tried to make enthusiastic that she was delighted, as she had thought Henry, at thirty-two, was a hopeless case, a confirmed bachelor. 'Now thank goodness, you have changed his mind. I am very happy. He needs looking after, he is no good at being a Nazi or a soldier for that matter. I only hope another awful war does not start, but we are not here to discuss that today. All I want to say to you is, Pamela dear, will you see that your dear mother and father come here to arrange the date of the marriage?'

Pig suddenly realised she had a new Christian name and could not call herself by her English nickname. It all seemed too good to be true and when she thought of persuading herself she was having a good time, she realised she was. She pinched herself to make sure she was going to be a princess and marry the man she loved, and live in the country. She jolly well would only have her sisters to stay once a year, although the children could come more often and she would put some colour into their cheeks.

She was too excited to sleep on the night train to Paris. Henry had come to see her off and kissed her gently on the lips in the corridor. She had reacted with passion and they stood holding each other, their mouths glued together, for two or three minutes before he got off the train.

He was so kind and gentle, nice not only to her, but to waiters and his father and mother. He had such quiet, friendly ways she could not imagine he would hurt anybody. He was nicer to her than anyone had ever been in all her life. If she dropped a handkerchief, he picked it up; in England she had picked up her sisters'.

Her father was amazed at her news. Her mother hardly dared to believe it. Her sister, Cosima, said in a small voice, 'Are you joking?' Cecily stared at her with an open mouth. Her sisters, and even her father frowned when she said she was becoming a Roman Catholic.

A few weeks later Pig returned to Berlin with her parents, and it was arranged that the marriage would take place in September. She was to have eight attendants, four boys and four girls. Cosima's son was one of the pages and Cecily's daughter a bridesmaid. All the rest were German princes and princesses whose names she could never remember.

Henry had been given two months' leave. To begin with they were going to Venice for the honeymoon. Afterwards they planned to stay in his favourite house in the woods near Rothenburg.

Pig seldom gave a thought to politics, although for years she had heard fears expressed that there would be another war. But during her stay in Germany Sir William Sanderson convinced her that Germany only wanted her own people to be well treated in other countries. Surely England and France would not fight to stop such a reasonable desire?

Her wedding dress was designed by Norman Hartnell. He pondered a long time before making a decision. Pig laughed. 'I am a bit square, aren't I?' He jumped. 'Oh no, not at all. How tall is your husband?' She said he was about six feet one while she was five foot eight. He stood upright on his tiny feet, made a wry face, but managed to get out, 'You will make a lovely bride.'

All went well at the marriage except that Cosima's little daughter cried all through the service. Pig was happy on their honeymoon because she loved looking after Henry. She ordered him new, long woollen underclothes because he said he was always cold in winter. He appeared to be happiest lying back in a gondola or sitting in a huge, hideous church called St Mark's. Many of his relations were still in Venice, the season was only just over and Pig, which she insisted her friends should call her – she never could remember who Pamela was! – found to her delight everyone appeared to be fond of Henry. Sometimes she wondered why he was so low-spirited but decided he was delicate; his sickliness made her even fonder of him. He seemed to her a different man after their marriage, as if the wedding had tired him out. He did not seem to mind a bit how much she danced at parties or who with, as long as he could sit with a friend, or in silence. After a riotous dance he always asked her politely if she had enjoyed herself. It was wonderful never to be criticised and always praised and cosseted. She did not care that they did not see any pictures or churches for she had always hated sightseeing and was delighted Henry felt the same way. She would have been bored to tears if he had wanted to tramp round museums and look at portraits which every-one went on about as if they were interesting people. How could they be interesting when they were dead? Her one regret was his lack of passion. Luckily she found out that orange and green dresses excited him. She decided to please him. The trouble in Venice was she could not find a single orange dress except in the cheapest shops!

When they arrived at his father's country house she was amazed to learn it was called 'The Bear's Cage': apparently some prince, hundreds of years before, had owned a pet animal with such strong personality that it was allowed to come to lunch and sit in its own huge chair – still there – with deep claw scratches in the solid wooden arms. The bear also had a large pewter bowl engraved with his name, the date of his birth, his death and how much he was regretted. She liked the house at once. It had three flat fronts surrounding a circular courtyard. Two wings extended from the northern front. The decoration of the rooms was based on the fashion which Queen Victoria's daughters had encouraged in Europe. Nearly every room had chintz curtains and padded wooden armchairs.

At the end of the first week Henry's father wrote to say he hoped they would live in an apartment in the north wing, facing the west. They could refurnish it in their own taste exactly as they liked. There were four bedrooms, two bathrooms, two sitting rooms, a kitchen and servants' halls. When Pig saw the faded chintzes and furniture which she was told had been made by a man called Beidermeister, she knew she did not wish to change anything. Her mother-in-law came down for a night to see they had everything they wanted and was delighted with her decision.

Pig loved driving and every day she and Henry drove round the countryside. It was full of old castles, none of them as nice as the Bear's Cage. All Henry's relations welcomed her and she could not make up her mind whether they liked her because she was now Princess Henry or because of her personality. She did not understand that they welcomed her because she looked and behaved like a Saxon peasant who could easily be moulded. Anything was better than a typical, badly dressed, upper class English woman who whispered in corners, seldom spoke and smiled in a superior way instead of laughing. Officers looked at her in the streets in a familiar way which was exciting. It wasn't at all the way Henry looked at her, but then Henry was Henry and she was confident she could change him.

In October she looked forward to visiting Berlin again, this time for a week of parties, when an unimagined event revolutionised her relationship with Henry. A book arrived by post from England. She couldn't think who it could be from as her family and friends never sent her books. The parcel was labelled 'Reading matter'. She looked at the postmark and was amazed to see it came from Aylesbury. She had no idea where it was and was sure she had never met anyone who came from there. Inside was a letter, loosely attached to the front cover of the book, written on writing paper headed 'House of Lords, Westminster, London W1'.

Dear Princess, I hope you will forgive this letter. I had intended sending it to you when your engagement was announced but my wife dissuaded me. The reason I take the liberty of writing is that I have always

147

admired your father's sense of Christian fairness in the House of Lords. I myself am a member. I am also a Jew.

You are now living in a country where Jews, for no fault of their own, are suffering cruel persecution. If you read this recently published book with an introduction by the Bishop of Durham, who verifies the horrifying facts related in it, you will, I hope, be shocked. I have taken the liberty of marking passages which have caused me, and will I hope cause you, distress. I have blacked out sections which I consider too disgusting for you to read.

Please forgive this letter. It is my belief the appalling truths published justify my sending it in case you are ignorant of them. Be careful you do not soon find yourself absorbed into a nation which intends to exterminate my people. Read the book and you will see I am not a madman but a worried Jew. I cannot tell you my name. My hope is you will be a good influence in Germany. Forgive my badly expressed letter.

From an English-Jewish patriot.

Amazed, Pig looked through the book, which was called *The Yellow Spot*, and was horrified at the cartoons of Jews cooking rats to make sausages, and tormenting German children. She began to read Chapter Five; a marked passage caught her eye:

STREICHER'S MODEL

The people hope one day to see the time
When shooting the last Jew will be no crime!

('Nursery Rhyme' from the Sturmer)

148

Pig was shocked, and her horror was increased by the chapter.

PALM SUNDAY IN GUNZENHAUSEN

Gunzenhausen is a small town in Franconia with old mediaeval walls and a pretty little Gothic church. It is a poor neighbourhood. Even during economic booms few of the blessings of modern times have penetrated to Gunzenhausen.

Petty trading with the neighbouring countryside is the main means of livelihood. In years of crisis, business is bad, life which is normally simple becomes hard and difficult, and the people ask why this should be so. The church, the authority round which till now their life had centred, can give them no satisfying answer. Then someone declares it is the Jews who are to blame. Follows the pogrom. Hatred of Jewish competition is no new emotion in Gunzenhausen; even after the mediaeval ghetto walls had fallen, in such peasant territories invisible barriers still remained.

This is the region with which Julius Streicher is linked by 'blood and soil'. He had made Franconia the 'model district'.

At the beginning of 1934 there were still nineteen Jewish families living in Gunzenhausen: tradesmen, handicraftsmen, innkeepers. Obviously these nineteen families could not live by dealing only with each other. A few 'Aryans' still bought from them, perhaps some of these went out of their way to do so to show their sympathy.

Gunzenhausen happens to be the home of the parents of Storm Trooper Leader Kurt Baer, a member of Julius Streicher's personal bodyguard.

Kurt Baer is one of the 'old fighters' of the National Socialist movement and had in the early days been implicated in one of the Feme murders committed by the infamous Heines. One day, visiting his native village, he heard criticisms of Hitler. 'You've all gone totally Jew!' was his answer. He would show what one day must be done.

Early on Palm Sunday 1934, Kurt Baer and his Storm Troop squad marched into Gunzenhausen. On this day is celebrated Christ's entry into Jerusalem and the streets were full of churchgoers. Kurt Baer, at the head of his squad, issued a few sharp commands. Detachments entered Jewish houses. Doors were broken in, a few shots fired and a number of windows smashed. The Jews were dragged from their houses, some of them from cellars to which they had fled in terror. Baer ordered them to be brought to his presence, and then his squad dragged them through the streets of the town. There was a great deal of noise and shouting. Some of the crowd withdrew, others followed the procession to the town hall. On the last part of the journey Squad Leader Baer himself dragged a Jewish woman behind him by the hair.

The ceremony was continued in the large hall of the municipal offices. The victims, including women-folk, were whipped and knocked about. Until the small hours of the morning, drinking, shouting and brutality continued. Next morning two corpses were found in Gunzenhausen. The seventy-five year old Jew, Rosenfelder, lay in the street with his chest torn open by knife wounds. The thirty-year old Jew, Rosenau, hung on a garden fence. Some of the victims had been detained in captivity. The remainder had crept home.

On Monday all the Jewish shops in the village were

closed. Not till late at night did the captain of the police appear.

The Gunzenhausen pogrom was not an isolated incident. It was only isolated in respect to the fact that, instead of being forgotten, news of it leaked across the Czech frontier. On April 3rd an account of the incident appeared in the *Manchester Guardian*. But Julius Streicher, Kurt Baer's chief, told English journalists (*Volkischer Beobachter*, 17th May, 1934) in Nuremburg:

'Gentlemen, I herewith most emphatically declare to you that not a single Jew has been murdered, nor has any Marxist been killed.'

She skipped some pages until her attention was caught by another quotation from *The Sturmer* – which she knew Henry's brother took – in the issue of August 1935 she read:

'Moreover, the Jew has in his veins a large element of Negro blood; his frizzy hair, his wolf lips, the colour of his eyeballs prove this as effectually as the insatiable sexual greed which hesitates at no crime and finds its supremest triumph in the brutal defilement of women of another race. This bestial lust obsesses even a barely mature Jew boy.. . .'

'A non-Jewish girl must be regarded as cattle is regarded.'

'A non-Jewish girl may be defiled as soon as she is three years and one day old . . .'

'This Jew (his name and address follow) belongs to the alien race that believes itself able to carry on its race defilement with impunity just as before. He is acting according to the Talmadic principles of his race. Jewesses are too good for his vileness. Accordingly he runs after non-Jewesses. Non-Jewesses are, according to the Talmud, to be regarded as cattle; the Jew can, therefore, defile and ruin them with an easy conscience.'

The next paragraph was blacked out. *The Yellow Spot* went on:

'These accusations were put in to justify the brutal persecution of the Jews.'

'*The Sturmer* sends men on to the streets to photograph women who happen to be talking to a Jew or entering a Jewish shop. These photographs are published with such letterpress as: "This young woman shopped at a Jew's shop; her husband is employed at the State Theatre", or:
"In the face of (name follows) is mirrored the shamelessness and lack of self-respect which have resulted in her from contact with a Jew. In the face of the Jew (name follows) gleams satanic joy."'
(Nos. 25 and 33, 1935)

The Sturmer publishes caricatures attended by verses of a revealing character:

> No real woman'd do that – would she now?
> For only a pig has dealings with a sow.

The next paragraph and a half had been blacked out.
Pig felt the hairs on her arms prickling with horror. She had often heard a lot of talk about the persecution of the Jews but it meant no more to her, until she went to Berlin, than accounts of Japanese murdering Chinese. She had

never seen any incidents then and Henry's friends had
made no comments on the subject except to say how the
British press seemed determined to run down the Führer.

The parcel had been brought to her as she sat, homesick
for England, in a wooden summer house which circulated
on wheels to follow the sun. It stood in an empty clearing
behind the kitchen garden, so scrupulously neat that, like
the ordered beds surrounding the house, it made Pig feel
untidy. She could not imagine how the footman had found
her and after a while felt disgusted and threw the book on
the floor. Surely a bishop would not support lies? She
looked at the yellow cover lying there, an enemy, and
fought back the wish to pick it up. It was no good. She
bent down and re-opened the pages. She had never been
clever but she could not help thinking the book was telling
the truth. The detailed evidence reminded her of the
reports she used to get in the East End of London about
the cases she was sent to tackle. The photographs surely
could not have been faked. Of course it was nothing to do
with Henry but it did seem as if well-known people in
Germany were determined to destroy a people she had
always rather looked down on; her family had always
avoided them in Sheffield, but she had never heard anybody suggest persecuting them. She thought of her husband's gentle, kind, sloping face and stood up. Perhaps he
did not know and – the thought came to her – if he did he
would use his influence to stop this sort of thing going on.
He could not approve of it, and he might be able to rebut
these accusations; she had never seen him kill a fly. Indeed,
his passivity worried her, and made him seem quiet and
lazy. She hoped he did not know what was happening to
the Jews and that once she had told him he would share
her feelings.

They had a quiet dinner together; the main dish was
white sausages, a present from a cousin in Munich. Henry

said they had not been boiled long enough. Opening a diary she made a note of his criticism and, hiding the book behind her back, went into the library and sat in her usual place. At precisely ten o'clock Henry looked at his watch. How he knew the exact time Pig never knew. But he would then stand up, examine the shutters, turn off the lights and silently lead Pig upstairs to bed. After he had undressed he would fold his clothes neatly, and without looking at her, take a book from his bedside table and start reading himself to sleep. He was not, to Pig's disappointment, despite her many orange dresses, a frequent lover. She often wondered if he had spent himself on their honeymoon. Before he started to read Pig leant over, took his hand and said in a nervous but determined voice, 'I read this book today about torturing Jews and imprisoning them in Germany. Is it true?'

Henry did not look at her but said, 'There is nothing I can do about it. Nothing at all. The Jews did much that I deplore. They thrived while the rest of Germany starved.' He had shut his eyes and she saw his body was stiff with annoyance.

'If what the book says is true, ought not you to do something?'

'There is nothing I can do, and if I did it would upset everything, and my brothers would be furious. This place might even be taken from us,' and to Pig's horror he burst into tears.

She tried to comfort him but he turned away and lay on his side, sobbing. 'There is nothing I can do, nothing.' She pressed herself against him, took his hand away from his face and held it firmly in hers, saying, 'My darling, I do not mean to worry you.' He continued to sob. She begged, 'Don't be unhappy. I only wondered if you knew. I don't really mind about these Jews, but for some silly reason I felt sorry for them this afternoon.'

Very slowly he disengaged his hand, turned round and laid his head on her shoulder. Pig patted him and put her arms around him as if he were a baby. She felt protective and loving as he relaxed in her arms. After a few moments he ceased to cry and said, 'I have always been useless. When I was a boy my younger brothers played games, rode, shot, and fenced better than I did. I was never any good at anything and when I went into the Army, I was only accepted as an officer because of my name. I wish I had not been. I am as bad at soldiering as I am at everything else. You know, it was not my father who suggested I gave up the titles and properties. I did not feel up to it and begged them to allow me to lead a quiet life. You have made me happy. When I am with you I do not feel I have to compete and can be my silent self, secure because you are and always will be with me. You have made up for my mother who always wanted me to succeed and, although she pretends, will never forgive my hopelessness.' He nestled against her shoulder.

Pig tried to analyse her thoughts. His breakdown made her feel protective and loving, but at the same time she was conscious of a feeling of disillusionment which made her realise, even when she was consoling him, that things would never be the same again. She would in future think of him not as a lover but as a child or a sick brother who had to be nursed. She wondered if she should have married him as he continued to go on about his difficulties.

'I think Hitler is a beastly madman, but my mother and brothers point out that Germany was degraded before he came, and there was poverty and starvation and now we are a rich country and everybody has enough to eat. But I don't know, all I know is that they will fight another war and kill more people. I hate it all but if I had left the Army they would have said I was a coward. I am not brave enough to admit that is true. I am not brave enough to come out on the side of the Jews as you suggest because my family would turn on me, and despite your strength I would give in to them as I always have. I don't know why, but I have never been able to stand up to my mother and I am still frightened of her, my only consolation is that I have you.'

She wished he would not go on exposing his weaknesses, and felt she must have been mad to fall in love with this sickly schoolboy.

Pig hugged him and decided that to save him she would have to support whatever he did without questioning whether it was right or wrong. The decision changed her life and character. She felt her love for Henry had died and been replaced by an insincere but passionate loyalty. At the same time she knew she would have to live a separate life or Henry would irritate her to death. One childish man was as much as she could deal with. The Jews would have to look after themselves.

Two weeks later in Berlin she began a love affair with a Prince Caralath-Bouthon. She had fun, felt physically satisfied and even more determined to look after Henry and become a good German. Her natural cheerfulness had won. Luckily the generals thought as little of Henry as he did of himself, and never thought of sending him to any front line. He was kept in training camps or doing ordnance work and was able to take frequent periods of leave. Pig was always kind to him.

She was able to communicate with her family through Switzerland; as the war went on she noticed her father's letters grew colder and colder until they merely gave her the brief details of her mother's health. She told herself she did not mind. One evening in September 1943, after a busy day in Rothenburg shopping and attending a Red Cross meeting, she made a tour of the kitchen garden now planted with vegetables, the paths ploughed up. The glasshouses were filled with tomatoes and only one vine had been left to provide Muscat grapes for the house. She picked a bunch, ate it and walked in a good temper back to the house only to find a letter from Cosima:

Pig, I can no longer keep quiet. Details have been published in the British papers of the massacre of Jews by a nation whose ambitions you have adopted. Have you gone mad? How can you write happily of a lovely day in the sun when Jews are being murdered in thousands in the most dreadful way? Do you know nothing, or have you changed? Do not write to me again if you have . . . Your sister Cosima.

P.S. My husband who is in the Army agrees with every word I have written.

Pig, sure Cosima's husband had dictated the letter, tore it into little pieces. She had never liked her sister and did not care if she never saw her again. But sitting down she felt tired and worried. Before the Red Cross meeting that afternoon she had heard two old First World War generals talking about the living conditions of Jews in the Krupps' factories. One of them had said, 'They are treated like mad dogs, starved, kept in kennels. Hundreds have died. Such a thing would never have happened in our time. I cannot believe it is right. Anyhow, such cruelty will not help us win a war which we are losing.' The other general nodded. 'I agree, things look bad.'

Pig had already heard of the Jews worked to death in Krupps' factories sleeping in dog kennels and hovels. But her loyalty to Henry had hardened her heart and she decided it was nothing to do with her. She looked angrily at the two old men, resenting their conversation. But she was worried about the outcome of the war. She had never contemplated that her new fatherland might be beaten. She shivered: what would happen to her if Germany was defeated? The next day her fears vanished, driven out of her head by a calamity. A telegram arrived saying Henry's father, his two younger sons and their wives and children had been killed in Frankhiem by a British bomb. Pig was horrified. She wished the bomb had not been British, and rushed over to comfort her mother-in-law who, the day before, had undergone a minor operation and lay in a district hospital, weak, sad and crying. Pig moved into the next room to nurse her night and day. Sometimes the older woman would go to sleep holding her hand, and Pig could not help thinking about her change of circumstance as the disaster meant that Henry would now have to become head of the family. This meant that instead of living in the wing of a house they would own castles galore including a palace in Berlin. She thought it was rather exciting and then how wicked she was not to be sad about the many deaths. She pulled herself together. Of course she was sorry about the bomb, but at the same time pleased that Henry would now become a great figure in Germany. She hoped the calamity would make a man of him.

Not for the first time she wished she could have a baby. Apparently it was possible, there was nothing wrong with her, nor him, except that he had what the doctor had called 'lazy sperm'. Anyhow, it was not her fault, there was nothing wrong with her body. She gave a little smile. There were other men in Germany except Henry. Immediately she blamed herself for immorality and made up her mind never to have another man's child.

She was a good nurse and her mother-in-law quickly felt better and was able to go and stay with relations. Henry had been to see her twice and Pig noticed he showed no sympathy for his mother who had shaken her head impatiently when he asked her politely how she was.

He was charming. He was hopeless. When Pig returned to the Bear's Cage the house seemed to have lost a part of its charm. She wondered why.

Four days later she was taking a morning walk in the woods when a voice said, 'Pig MacIntosh'. She almost jumped out of her skin as a man stepped on to the path and took off his hat. He was dressed in German clothes and wore a grey overcoat and a green hat with jays' feathers stuck in the brim. She vaguely recognised his freckled face and fair hair. 'Pig MacIntosh,' he repeated. 'I am going to be quick, for, to say the least of it, it would be inconvenient if we were interrupted. I have been here for twelve days. Let me tell you why. You know that the Schloss Lowenberg, which is only a few miles from here, is being used to imprison Jewish eggheads who are not useful to the Germans? You did not know? Well, it is. One of the prisoners is a mathematical genius, four are scientists who work in a laboratory, two are writers and four are Jews who are fortunate enough to have money abroad; a large sum is paid annually on condition they are kept alive. The four scientists are very useful to the Germans. They are all willing to escape to Switzerland and it is my business to plan the route. I entered Germany from the Swiss border and with help have arranged three hiding places where I hope they will be safe on the way out. You can provide the first. Unfortunately your husband has so much land it is impossible not to involve you in this neighbourhood. One of our helpers came up with the perfect place: you can reach it if you continue down this path until you reach a quarry, closed down years ago. In it is a large cave. As it was exceptionally dry, an internal store room and offices and even a lavatory were put in before the First World War. Since then it has never been used, but the Nazis inspect it twice a year in March and September. It was inspected last week. Our information is that it is in perfect order. We plan to release the prisoners on Wednesday fortnight. They may have to stay two or three days until the immediate fuss dies down. I was told to approach you by old friends of yours in England who believe you will help. The risk to you is, I believe, minimal. All I ask you is to ensure your gardeners and grooms do not by any chance go down to the quarry from Wednesday to Saturday. You might ride in a different direction each day and see that they are kept busy. You need know nothing more. Remember, the lives of eleven men are at stake. The reason we have to stop is that we can move our party between one and five o'clock in the morning when the patrols relax. We also do not wish to use cars from outside their own neighbourhood.'

He handed her a sheet of paper. 'I understand our minister used to know you. He sends you his respects. I know I can rely on you. In an emergency leave a message saying "Teresa cannot lunch with Claus Hoffman at the Hotel Goethe in Frankfurt". Goodbye.'

He turned and disappeared into the wood. She racked her brains but could not remember who he was or where she had met him, but as she walked into her front door she remembered it had been at a ball in Londonderry House. He was wearing tails and dancing with a girl with long black hair. She had liked his intelligent face and asked who he was. They were introduced, she remembered he lived in Wiltshire and was going the next day to learn farming with an uncle in Kenya. She had felt vaguely disappointed but had soon forgotten him. The old incident encouraged her to have faith in his plan and at the same time eased her conscience about the Jews.

During the last two years she had never met a soul in the woods, the foresters and keepers had all been called up to serve in the Army, the old ones to work in nearby factories. On Monday and Tuesday she walked to the quarry. All was quiet. She took two of her husband's dogs who barked at shadows and never stopped looking for rabbits. Nobody was about.

Two weeks later on the vital Wednesday morning Henry sent a telegram to say he was returning late that evening on unexpected leave. When he arrived Pig was at first pleased to see him. But her attempts to amuse him were unsuccessful. He smiled politely, kissed her and went and looked out of the window. She asked him what was wrong. When he shook his head she noticed his face was grey. Immediately she felt guilty. Had she, by agreeing to the man's plans, added to his worries? She cursed the Jews. She had never liked them and now they seemed to be causing her complications. Dinner was no fun, Henry sat silent, took small helpings, pushed them aside, sighed.

After dinner he sat down by the fire and without picking up a book or a newspaper closed his eyes. Pig was worried. He had often been dreary, but never as dreary as this. She went and sat on the arm of his chair and pulled his head towards her. 'What is it? I must know. You've got to tell me. You cannot go hanging about looking as if you are going to die.' 'Perhaps I am,' he said in a lugubrious voice. He paused, waited a moment. 'You know, ever since Wilhelm was arrested and Henry died in an aeroplane, or was shot, which of course he was, Hitler has become suspicious of everybody. I saw Max yesterday and he told me there is no doubt that the Führer intends to liquidate all members of the old ruling families that have any status. From now on, if any excuse can be found, we will be thrown into prison and killed.' He sighed again.

Pig felt dizzy with guilt. Usually she was bored and irritated when he was downcast and unhappy. But the idea that she might have endangered his life at a difficult time brought back an echo of her love, and an overwhelming feeling of guilt. Perhaps, or because of, her free life, she wanted for him to be calm and happy. Pig was still at heart a kind, simple girl. After all, he allowed her to do what she liked and had changed her from a dull spinster into a princess. Whatever happened she was not going to let him down. Should she stop the Jews using the quarry? Pig looked at Henry's sad face. Her duty was clear; she would ring Hoffman and tell him he was forbidden to come. She rang his hotel and left a message 'Teresa is unable to lunch with Herr Hoffman'. Had she heard breathing down the telephone? Well, if she had, the listener would have learned nothing except a banal message.

II

Pig was correct in thinking her conversation was overheard but she was unaware her telephone had been tapped in the Bear's Cage ever since her marriage. As she was the daughter of a British minister it was thought possible that even if she was not a British sympathiser she might be a source of useful information on the views of the British government. The listeners had never heard any information of the slightest importance. After a year they had reported that the princess appeared never to exchange political information with her father. Her war-time conversations had been equally innocent. Then came her overheard telephone call to Hoffman. The hotel manager was told to observe his movements.

Actually the Gestapo had already picked up 'Hoffman' as he had the unfortunate habit of singing in his bath, and one morning had sung half the first verse of the Winchester Marching song before he remembered where he was and stopped dead. A housemaid heard him and reported her suspicions to the contact to whom she had to report. Consequently Hoffman was followed before he saw Pig and his escape plan guessed by the Gestapo – and confirmed when his parked car was spotted near the quarry.

The Gestapo chief rang up Berlin and explained his dilemma. What was he to do? Should he interrogate the princess? Was Hoffman to be arrested? A reply came, 'Do nothing but watch both carefully and, of course, tap his telephone.'

As Pig's message was not given to Hoffman he went on with his plan to pick up his human cargo and take them to the quarry. Meanwhile the Gestapo made preparations to meet him. Two platoons of the SS were sent from a nearby base, and, under the command of the efficient Shiner, arrived at the quarry at six o'clock on Wednesday evening. His platoon brought with them two long poles, spades, a coil of thick wire and bottles of spirits.

It rained on Thursday and Pig sat listening to her best friend, Anna Wilhelmburg, a fat, talkative, passionate young woman whose life was ruled by jealousy of her younger sister Helena, who put her in the shade by riding, talking and dancing with an ability which made Anna feel clumsy and uninteresting; above all she was prettier. Recently Helena had written a book which had been received with enthusiasm and acclaimed as a feminine twentieth century 'Young Werther'. That her sister should succeed in public had driven Anna into a frantic rage and she had decided to make Pig her private dependent and ordered her, if she ever had a spare minute, to ring her up and she would come over. Pig was grateful but was a little embarrassed by Anna's overwhelming attention and endless conversation. She liked talking herself but was seldom allowed to get a word in.

They had just finished eating lunch and as usual Pig was listening to Anna, hoping she would go before long when the door opened and Henry came tottering in, ignored Anna, and begged Pig in an imploring voice, to come with him. They went out, clinging together. Anna did not dare follow.

Pig begged Henry to tell her what had happened. He shook his head and walked on through the main house and along the kitchen corridor until they came to the estate office. Two Gestapo officers jumped to their feet, clicked their heels, bowed.

When Berlin had heard of the princess's involvement in the escape the subject was considered so delicate that the matter was reported by Himmler to the Führer who lost his temper and shouted he would use Pig's treachery as an excuse for having the remaining Rothenburgs shot. Himmler advised caution. The district was loyal to the family and the present Duke's father had been loyal to the Nazis from 1934 until his recent death. The family calamity had made the weak Henry a martyr and the name was still highly respected in the district. Himmler continued: 'In my view, taking into consideration the position of the family, it would be wiser to give the prince and princess a severe fright. I suggest that Hoffman should be allowed to escape with the Jews. When they arrive at the quarry they and the collaborators will be hung. The punishment of Hoffman will be left to those who can be trusted.

'Photographs of the executed Jews will then be shown by Major Shiner to the prince and princess. I think this will ensure their future loyalty.' Hitler shrugged his shoulders. The plan was put in motion.

Shiner did not speak until the terrified couple had sat down opposite him, then he cleared his throat and said, 'I am aware of the princess's meeting with a man calling himself Hoffman two weeks ago. (Henry gave his wife a horrified look.) The German Intelligence have followed him since he crossed the Swiss frontier. All his calls had

164

been overheard including his conversation with the princess.' He bowed politely to Pig who thought she was going
to faint.

As the Major continued she noticed the whites of his
eyes were yellow. Why, she wondered. 'All these facts,' he
went on, 'have been reported to the Führer, who was
relieved when the princess, doubtless re-assessing the
situation, had refused to work with her late countryman
and commit an act of treachery against the interests of her
husband's family.' The Major turned his eyes on Henry,
who feebly nodded his head. 'In fact the princess has
enabled our men to welcome Hoffman and the escaping
party in the quarry.' He produced an envelope, opened it,
stood up, walked around the table and laid a bunch of
photographs before Pig. 'Please look at these.' She pulled
herself together and examined the quarry with two high
wooden poles driven into the ground. Between them on a
stretch of thick wire hung sixteen men, their necks
extended, their bodies hanging at different angles. 'Please
study them,' said the Major. But she could not look.
However, Henry, anxious to please, leaned forward and
one by one placed the photographs in front of her. One of
the photographs showed a military truck standing under-
neath the gallows while SS men attached their victims to
the line. Pig glanced at the photographs for a second but
immediately looked away. The last photograph Henry laid
out was of Hoffman lying on his back, his nose broken,
two black eye holes in his head. A thin iron bar lay on the
ground by him. Behind him a man stood smiling.

Henry prodded his wife in the back. She wanted to
scream, but he leaned forward and whispered, 'Control
yourself, remember you are married to me.' She managed
to sit still and stop herself from crying. She heard the
Major rise to his feet, salute and say before leaving the
room, 'The Führer has asked me to thank you for your

collaboration in this affair which, as you have seen, resulted in this extermination of traitors to your – ' he stressed the word ' – country.'

Henry led her to her bedroom. She told him to get rid of Anna and lay down and sobbed for a week. He visited her twice a day and asked politely how she was. It was announced that she had 'flu. After a week of despair her spirits began to revive. Anna called incessantly, determined to find out what had happened and when she had broken Pig down, told her how lucky she had been and that never, never again should she think of helping the Jews who were meeting the fate they deserved. She would give her books to prove what they had done to Germany. And it was not only herself that Pig had to think about, or Henry, but the whole of German royalty whose lives she had endangered by her stupidity in listening to an Englishman so stupid that he even sang in his bath in Rothenburg. Pig must remember she was by marriage a German and learn and listen to the truth and, thank God, she had realised her stupidity in time and been loyal to Germany.

Anna's strong character made Pig feel better. She quickly recovered her natural high spirits as the effects of the photographs wore off.

She was amazed how quickly she was welcomed in England by Henry's cousins when the war was over. And went out of her way after 1945 to be pleasant to Jews, feeling she was redressing wrongs Hitler had inflicted on them in the war. She never allowed herself to feel guilty. After all, as she put it, 'I was in the same bus as the Pope and the Red Cross. That was good company.'

Henry is still alive but it is doubtful if he is aware of the fact.